A DEAD
COLLECTION

when truth rivals fiction, all bets are off

KENT FRATES

THE ROADRUNNER PRESS
OKLAHOMA CITY, OKLAHOMA

The RoadRunner Press
Oklahoma City, Oklahoma
www.TheRoadRunnerPress.com

Bulk copies or group sales of this book available by
contacting: orders@theroadrunnerpress.com.

FIRST EDITION DECEMBER 2022

Printed in the USA

The following stories and poems were previously published, as follows:
"Father's Day," *Cowboy Jamboree Magazine,* Fall 2017
"Uncle Earl," *Red Dirt Forum*, Issue 1, Winter 2018
"A Dubious Collection," *Red Dirt Forum*, Issue 2, Fall 2018
"Piano Player," *Red Dirt Forum*, Issue 4, Spring 2020
"Ghosts," *Red Dirt Forum*, Issue 4, Spring 2020

10 9 8 7 6 5 4 3 2 1

*Sulful Spring Wonderful
Friend!*

This book is dedicated to Kurt, Lloys, and Cole,
who have had to put up with me their entire lives.

*thankyou for
being a wonderful
friend + sharing
you + your
husband!*

Susan Bootlke

A
DUBIOUS
COLLECTION

truth or fiction, we'll never tell

TABLE OF CONTENTS

THE STORIES

THE POEMS

FOR TRUTH IS ALWAYS STRANGE,
STRANGER THAN FICTION.

—LORD BYRON,
BRITISH POET AND SATIRIST

EVIL KNIEVEL

. . . .

Evil Knieval was a true outlaw in the best sense of the word—not some phony country singer who calls himself that just because he drinks too much or smokes dope. Evil was the real McCoy, an icon who went from stealing motorcycles to jumping his motorcycle over everything from cars to rattlesnakes.

He was known as much for his failures as his successes.

He was honest too. He said it wasn't true that he had broken every bone in his body, only forty.

A natural born showman, Evil turned himself into a red-white-and-blue legend. Born to fly, and crash, and ride again, he probably would have rather have died some spectacular death, as he almost did once, hurtling across eighteen fountains at Caesars Palace in Las Vegas on his bike. But he didn't die then and now he's gone anyway, and we should mourn, not so much for Evil, as for what he was: Someone who led his life his own way and damn the consequences.

WHAT DID THEY SAY
· · · · · · · · · · · ·

We were on our way to Beaver, Oklahoma, even though no one goes there on purpose. That's not quite true, as there was at least one good reason for a trip to this windswept, rural town, staked far out in the Oklahoma Panhandle.

No, we weren't going for the cow chip throwing contest, even though that figured in the reason for our trip. No, what caused us to drive halfway across the state on this spring day was a chance to meet with State Senator Billy Butts. The Boss needed his help and Butts's secretary at his legislative office in Oklahoma City had made it quite clear the only chance to see the Senator for months would be to catch him in Beaver on the Saturday of the town's annual World Cow Chip Throwing Contest. Otherwise, she couldn't promise an appointment until after the legislative session was over and that was too late for what we needed, which had put us in the Boss's big Cadillac Escalade speeding west through miles and miles of nothing but miles and miles. *He had a lot of power and a lot of leverage and he knew it, and the Boss needed his help.*

This was big country. Open plains stretched all the way to the horizon in every direction, cast against a big sky, broken only occasionally by a windmill, a grain elevator, or an oil rig. In early spring everything still looked dead, an endless brown landscape of dormant grass and wheat that either hadn't grown yet or never would. If it hadn't been for the revival of the oil and gas business this whole part of the state, racked by one of the worst prolonged droughts since the 1930s, would have dried up and blown away. If you were a farmer or rancher who didn't have any oil production, you were either broke or going broke, done in by an endless string of days that brought only clear, cloudless skies and a relentless wind. Times weren't as bad as during the Dust Bowl days thanks to soil conservation and water resource development, but they were still plenty hard.

It took a tough breed of people to live in this country, and Billy Butts was one of them, through and through. The legendary senator grew up on a hard scrabble farm in Beaver County. Reared by his grandparents, he had managed a scholarship to Southwestern State College and then worked his way through law school at night in Oklahoma City, before opening a law office in Beaver.

Most people end up doing whatever they do in life as much by chance as by choice, but Butts knew what he wanted, and as it turned out, was born for the job. He was a professional talker. He could spin a yarn, charm a woman, or sway a jury, and when it came to politics, he was a natural. He once told a colleague that he was proud to say that he had made a good living all his life based on "pure bullshit." Butts could pile it high and deep, and make people like it.

Butts's success was not achieved without controversy. A damage suit lawyer, he had won some big judgments against corporations and insurance companies but had developed a reputation for playing fast and loose with the truth. He'd also run into a little trouble with the federal government and been prosecuted for income tax evasion. This charge resulted in a notorious trial in which Butts testified in his own behalf and so charmed the jury that, to the consternation of the U.S. attorney, Butts was found not guilty. All of which only enhanced his reputation as a clever and powerful political force.

Butts was also a master of political patronage and an expert in obtaining state jobs, welfare benefits, or government subsidies for his constituents. More importantly from our point of view was his chairmanship of the Senate Committee on Roads and Highways, through which he controlled what projects got funded and what did not. He had a lot of power and a lot of leverage and he knew it, and the Boss needed his help.

A real estate developer, the Boss had recently bought land to start a residential addition near Altus. The Altus Air Force Base was expanding; the town was growing; and things were looking good for this dusty town in the southwest corner of the state. That is, until, the proposed widening of the state highway that ran from town past the development appeared to fall through. Planned for years, the road-widening now looked as if the funding for it would never get out of the state legislature. If the road wasn't widened, the development was in danger and the Boss would be stuck with a lot of sorry pastureland and a big mortgage he might not be able to handle. The only man who could help was the venerable Senator Billy Butts.

Part Irish and part Kiowa Indian, the Boss was a feisty little man with a love for racehorses, cards, and golf. He had made and lost several fortunes in real estate development but remained a gambler at heart. The man could not resist plunging in when times looked good; he was the eternal optimist who thought good times would last forever. He was presently riding the latest oil boom, having hit a financial home run with a high dollar development near Oklahoma City. With nary a blink, he had immediately bought up land near Altus for a housing addition, plunging all of his profits into this new deal.

My job had become available due to the Boss's bad luck. After a late night card game at his country club, the Boss had garnered a DUI that caused him to lose his driver's license. Just out of high school and looking for a job myself, my situation had led a friend to refer me to the Boss who now needed a driver. The job mostly entailed driving him around but sometimes I was pressed into service, caddying or running errands.

Like most gamblers, the Boss didn't mind spending money when he had it and often handed me extra cash at such times, particularly after a good day at the track. Being around him didn't seem much like a job to me, even though the hours were long and erratic, and he demanded instant service. Giving up my Saturday to drive him some place, even Beaver, Oklahoma, wasn't all that unusual.

As we approached the town, he pointed out a large house under construction, a big two-story job with pillars in front, sort of a faux Southern mansion. The Boss speculated that it probably belonged to some local oilman or a farmer with a bunch of oil wells on his property. In any event, the place was clearly unusual for a town as small and ordinary as Beaver.

In town, we found the park where the cow chip throwing contest was in progress and pulled in near a line of pickup trucks. The contest site could have been a scene out of a Breughel painting. Kids were running, playing, and tossing Frisbees. Families clustered around charcoal fires, cooking and drinking beer. Music poured from cars and boom boxes and you could smell hamburgers cooking on a grill. The ground was so typically Beaver dry that the movements of people sent puffs of dust flying away on the wind, another reminder of the tough times at hand.

Across the park, the cow chip throwing contest was starting and some participants were already hurling a few chips. It looked like choosing the right chip was going to be important to a good throw, not too dry and for sure not too wet. A big pile of the chips was stacked near the throwing spot and a lot of trash talking was being exchanged as the competitors picked out their chips.

The contest was ironic, given the history of the high plains of the Oklahoma Panhandle. Originally, the buffalo had roamed the plains in great numbers, providing food and clothing for the Indian tribes that crisscrossed the area, living off of what must have seemed liked endless herds to them. The white-man proved that wrong on his arrival, killing off the buffalo, mostly for the hides, and then driving off the Native Americans too.

Vast cattle ranches followed next, using this sea of grass to graze thousands of head of cattle until they were displaced by a waive of farmers duped into inhabiting this arid land by the railroads and real estate promoters, and spurred on by the government's offer of free land. These nesters led an ill-fated adventure into dry land wheat farming, scalping the land by plowing up the native grasses and planting wheat, which only grew until the inevitable dry years hit, and the crops withered and the naked soil driven by the all-powerful winds swept across the land creating lethal dust storms. Storms so bad, that of those few souls who stayed, many died of dust pneumonia if starvation hadn't already claimed them.

During those dreadful Dust Bowl days, the settlers who hung on in the Oklahoma Panhandle burned cow chips for fuel until they ran out. Now here they were throwing them for sport in what seemed an historical mockery of the country's past. On the other hand, maybe cow chip throwing was a fitting memorial to the rough humor that those survivors of the Great Depression and the dust storms must have possessed to make it through one of our country's cruelest periods.

But on this day, the cow chip contest was not our concern. We had come to see the local Oracle even though Beaver bore no resemblance to Delphi, or any place else that might have a mountain or even a hill. To no surprise, the sky was cloudless and the day warm for the time of year. A few trees cast some shade, and it was under one of them that we spotted the Oracle himself, sitting in a lawn chair.

Senator Billy Butts was a big, loose-jointed man. He looked to be in his fifties, running a little to fat but still strong. He wore a white dress shirt, suspenders, cowboy boots, and a straw cowboy hat. He was treating the shady spot under the tree as his office and was talking to a rough-looking farmer, dressed in overalls, as we approached. He finished their conversation, shook the man's hand with a big smile, slapped him on the back, and waved us over. The Boss introduced himself and identified me as his employee.

"What can I do you boys for?" Butts inquired.

"We need to talk to you about a road and your secretary said this was the best time," the Boss said.

"All road leads to Rome but which one is it that you have in mind?" Butts inquired.

"That would be the state highway north of Altus," the Boss said.

"Mighty fine country down there," Butts said. "Those people are the salt of the earth. Now if my memory serves me right, you are a developer and your development is near that highway."

"Your memory serves you just fine," the Boss said.

"How are the folks making out down there? I know it's been drier than a popcorn fart. Do you reckon that part of the state will pull through this drought?"

"Well, we've been through it before and survived. The oil business helps."

"People out here in western Oklahoma are like ticks. No one understands how ticks survive the winter, but by God, they always do," Butts responded.

"I guess that's right," the Boss said.

"What is there about your road that makes it different from any other road in the state? Is it a pearl among swine, or just another swine?"

"It would be good for economic development and give better access to the Air Force base. The government's expanding the base and spending millions. They're going to bring in more people who'll need a place to live. The town is going to boom!"

A rivulet of sweat appeared from under the Senator's hatband and began to run down his forehead. He took a handkerchief from his pocket, wiped the sweat away, and signaled to a young boy standing nearby. The youngster hurried toward us. "Bobby, how about getting us three lemonades. It's hot out here and we need to wet our whistles." It was not a question, and the young boy did not take it as one. He scurried away to do the Senator's bidding.

"Well, now let me tell you about the youth of today. A lot of people complain about young people; they see these gang members, punks with tattoos, rings in their nose and their belly button, even in their nipples, I'm told. What I see around here are these good country folks and their kids. They raise their kids right. What do you think about that?"

"Well, Senator, it takes all kinds," the Boss said.

"Yes, but you can't make a racehorse out of a plow horse. That's something every farmer knows and every politician ought to know, but a hell of a lot of them don't."

As his words hung in the air, the kid returned with the three lemonades. The Senator handed him a ten dollar bill. "Bobby, here's for the lemonade; keep the change."

Butts then turned to us and said, "You know, this boy's family are fine people. Very fine people, they have always supported me in my elections. Poor, but they work hard and they're honest and this boy works hard and he's honest. Aren't you, Bobby?"

"Yes Sir, Senator."

"And you and your folks go to church on Sunday, don't you?"

"Yes, Sir."

"Ya see, that's what I'm talking about. The youth of today is the future of tomorrow. Thanks, Bobby." The boy then turned and left.

"Did you boys come into town from the east?"

"That's right, Senator," the Boss said.

"Well, you probably saw my house there, that house that was under construction, right as you got to town. You know, a man's home is his castle and everybody needs a place to call their own. I was born poor, but I've worked hard and been lucky, and now I'm going to have a nice place to call my own."

"It sure is, Senator," the Boss said.

"I've got me a good contractor. Bet you know the fella, he's from down in Oklahoma City, calls his company Gold Medal. *Gold Medal*, I like that."

"Why yes, I know him, Senator. I believe practically everybody in the state knows him. He's a big builder."

"Yes, but he's not cheap, no sir. He is not cheap."

"That's true," the Boss said.

"But, you get what you pay for in life, you always get what you pay for," Butts said.

"That's been my experience too, Senator," the Boss said.

"As nice as that house is goin' be, there is one thing that seems to be missing," the Senator said.

"And, what would that be?" the Boss asked.

"Growing up, you know, I thought that anybody that had their own swimming pool meant that they were rich. If you owned your own swimming pool, you would have everything that a person could ever want in this world. You could go swimming anytime you wanted, just go outside and jump in your own swimming pool. Wow, that's as good as it gets, owning your own swimming pool."

The Senator paused and took a long swallow of his lemonade; he gazed off into the distance as though calling up memories of his youth. "Now, you know down there in the legislature we only have so much money. We would like to spread a little bread upon the waters, all across the state. But we only have so much bread. It's just not enough to spread everywhere. Why, there must be dozens of roads like yours that need funding and there's people like you, that come to see me and they all have got a good reason why they need their road. I expect your reason is good, but their reasons are good too. What am I to do, when I go to my committee and ask them which roads we should pay for, every senator, he wants his road. He'll argue up and down for it. Your senator already has. It's hard to decide. Sometimes it wears me out thinking about it," Butts said.

"Well, Senator, I know it's hard to decide but you understand with that Air Force base down there, Altus is a hot spot for development and the road would be good for the whole state."

"You see, what I mean, you've got a good reason for that road. It's as good as any other reason. Problem is that it may not be any better than any other reason, just one of many good reasons, good reasons everywhere. I just wish that there was enough money for every good reason and every good road, but there's just not." Before the Boss could commiserate anymore about the lack of money for all the good reasons and roads, a man in a white shirt and tie approached. He looked to be a local official and he sounded official when he spoke. "Senator, it's your turn. The folks are waiting on you."

Senator Butts heaved himself up from his chair and said, "Well, I've got to go and throw a cow chip. The folks all get a kick out of it, makes for plenty of jokes too. A politician slinging shit, what else is new? You boys are welcome to stay around for the barbecue."

"Thank you, Senator, but we need to get back to the City," the Boss said.

"Thanks for coming, and by the way, I'll consider your reason and your road. Have a nice trip home," said Butts as he ambled off toward the contest area, the official-looking man trailing behind in the dust Butts was throwing up.

As for us, we got in the car and started back for Oklahoma City. Driving back through town, nothing about the place looked the least bit new or prosperous. The town wasn't exactly dying but it didn't look like a whole lot of living was going on either. When we got to the Senator's house, I took a little longer look than I had before. It was a fine looking place, being built with the best materials, obviously expensive. The Boss was quiet for a long time but finally said, "Corny old bastard, isn't he?"

"You got that right, Boss. I'm sorry you couldn't convince him about the road. I guess we wasted a trip."

"On the contrary, now we know the price of tea in China," the Boss said.

"Crap, Boss, now you're even talking like the Senator. What does that mean?"

"We know what it's going to take to get our road. Looks to be expensive though," the Boss said.

"What are you talking about? What do you mean *expensive*?"

"Well, it depends on the price of swimming pools," the Boss said.

21

A DUBIOUS COLLECTION

· · · · · · · · · · · ·

This story is for Steve. He was my friend. You can't have too many of those. He died of cancer thirty years ago. He never had a chance. He tried radiation and chemotherapy. They didn't work. Then he tried God, but it was too late for that too.

Perhaps, Steve took some consolation in having grown up unlike most of us. For one, he had a chauffeur. Well, not exactly a chauffeur, more like a surrogate father or one of those kindly butlers you see in old movies. Steve's dad was busy running a worldwide oil well drilling company and his mom, for some inexplicable reason, did not drive. So, Steve's dad hired a black man named Millage, and Millage drove Steve. No, that's not quite right: Millage raised Steve. Steve grew up a little wild and a lot of fat. He loved to eat, and he could always convince Millage that he had need of some ice cream or a hamburger even when his parents wanted their son to lose weight.

Millage drove Steve. No, that's not quite right: Millage raised Steve.

Steve's family owned a Chrysler Town & Country sedan. You may not remember the Town & Country. A cross between a station wagon and a two-door sedan, the vehicle was the post-World War II sequel to the woodie wagon; it looked like a sedan but got its name from its wooden double-doors. The one Steve's family owned had dynaflow, a cross between a standard and automatic transmission. Millage always drove Steve in the Town & Country.

As for Steve, he was a shrewd fella. I knew it and his close friends knew it. Unfortunately, his teachers didn't know it. Steve was a little allergic to school and his grades showed it, but he sure knew how to work Millage. Millage seemed to like his job. He tried to please his employers and knew the way to their hearts was through Steve. If Steve was pleased so were the bosses. If Steve was upset so were the bosses. So, Steve had Millage by the balls, and being a clever twelve-year-old, Steve knew it.

How did Steve use this upper hand? He spent it on the keys to that Town & Country, so he could drive the automobile all over the acreage where his family lived, out past the end of town. I don't know exactly what Steve said to Millage to secure this, but when his folks were out of town, the keys were always left where Steve could find them and Millage always looked the other way.

Try to picture a chubby boy, who could barely reach the gas pedal and still see over the steering wheel, gunning that old Town & Country down the red dirt back roads of Oklahoma with dust flying and the radio blaring rock and roll from XERF, a station out of Del Rio, Texas. I can because I was with him many a night. I still get a thrill thinking about tearing through the night in that big car, doing something we sure as hell weren't supposed to be doing and loving every illicit minute of it. How could Steve not be my friend for life, and he was. That's why I say this story is for Steve.

The story is true, but I don't think that really matters.

At the time that the story starts, I was hacking out a living trying to start a law practice on my own, taking any case that walked in the door. Steve worked for his dad's oil company. The company had high powered law firms to handle their legal work but Steve would send me any business he could. When my phone rang and I heard "Hello, Hollywood," I knew it was Steve calling. Ever since I went to college at Stanford, Steve had taken to calling me Hollywood. I don't know if his geography was confused or if he thought everyone from California was the same kind of nut.

"What can I do for you, Steve?"

"I got trouble in Creek County and I need a lawyer."

"If you've got trouble in Creek County you need a gun or a knife—to hell with the lawyer."

"Very funny, Counselor, I guess I'll just call a real lawyer instead of some kid barely out of law school."

"Well, you can't afford a real lawyer so tell me what you need."

"I pulled pipe on a well in Creek County and sold it to a guy to use as the framework for a building. He paid me some money down but still owes me the rest and says he can't pay. The company lawyer says I may be able to file some kind of lien on the property. Is that right?"

"It's called a materialmen's lien. It depends on the time since you furnished the pipe. Let me ask you a few questions. Who is this guy? How much does he owe you? And when exactly did you furnish him the pipe?"

"His name is M.C. Hopper. He owes me $12,000 and the pipe was delivered about two months ago."

"What kind of building is it, Steve?"

"Well, don't tell my wife, but it's a cockfighting pit."

"A what?"

"Cockfighting! You know what that is."

"How did you ever run on to this ol' boy?"

"I own roosters and go to the fights."

"I don't believe it."

"Well, Nancy thinks I sold them all. She'd kill me if she knew I still went to the fights and owned roosters."

"Get your paperwork and come on down, and we'll see if you can file a lien."

Steve showed up and I prepared the lien, and then I rushed off to Sapulpa, the county seat of Creek County, to file on the property. In the meantime, Steve reluctantly told me more about Hopper. Seems Hopper was an ex-con who had built the biggest cockfighting pit in the world near the town of Kellyville in Creek County. He and Steve had fought chickens at meets all over the state, and according to Steve, Hopper's word was good and, in spite of the debt, they were still on friendly terms.

Collection of my friend's debt suddenly didn't sound very promising to me, but I figured the lien might work, if it wasn't behind too many mortgages. I sent a copy of the lien to Hopper and got busy working on a nasty divorce case. I largely forgot about Steve's problem until one of the biggest men I'd ever seen exploded through my office door several days later. The intruder stood at least six-feet, five-inches tall and weighed easily more than three hundred pounds mostly, sadly for me, muscle. He was dressed in blue jeans, a faded shirt, and high-top work boots.

"Are you the lawyer who filed that lien for Steve on my property," he boomed. Having been threatened before in my office, I was awful glad to see him holding out his huge paw to shake hands as he said this. Based on the gesture, I confessed that I was, indeed, the lawyer in question.

"I'm M.C. Hopper and I'm a friend of Steve's. I can't pay him now but I need his help and so I need to talk to you."

And talk he did—or more accurately double-talk. Hopper it turned out was the world's greatest double-talker. He could talk for hours and never say a thing or say both sides to the same thing. If there was a point to what he said, only he seemed to know it. However, when finished, he'd look at the listener in a conspiratorial way as though he'd just revealed the secret of the ages and everyone was in agreement.

As best I could tell from what he told me, he was in a dispute with his construction contractor who had also filed a lien on his place. He thought the contractor was a crook and insisted he had forged Hopper's name to a document. Hopper wouldn't pay the contractor, so the contractor had walked off the job leaving Hopper to finish it himself. He wanted Steve to loan him money to finish the job and said he would pay Steve out of the proceeds from the next Big Meet, whatever that meant.

This was the gist of his message to me. In the course of receiving it, however, I heard about his views on cockfighting, prison, the criminal justice system, lawyers, and politics. His conversation pinged from subject to subject without a pause. His presence was overpowering and his nonstop delivery, suffocating. He told me he was now on his way to talk to Steve, and being sure that Steve would loan him the money, I could "paper it up." He then abruptly left, still mumbling something as he stormed out the door.

* * * * *

Steve called to tell me that sure enough he was loaning Hopper another $5,000 and that he would get paid when they had the Big Meet. I gave Steve my best lawyerly advice, which was: Don't do it even though it's only chicken feed to you. Steve called me a wiseass and said to draw up a note for Hopper, and I did.

Once again, I returned to other matters and set aside any thoughts of Steve or his lien. Or I did, until Steve called to tell me he was being sued. This time it wasn't his buddy Hopper but rather trouble by way of the big man himself. Seems Steve had been named as a party in a suit filed by the contractor to foreclose on the lien he'd filed on Hopper. M.C. had then hired an attorney who doubled as the state senator for Creek County, a man notorious for having taken a bribe in an airplane for his vote in favor of a bill to legalize gambling on horse races. Although there was little doubt that the state senator had taken the money, the case was dismissed because the prosecutor could not prove what state the plane was flying over at the time of the bribe. The Senator escaped prosecution for lack of jurisdiction. Much speculation ensued as to whether the Senator had been clever enough to arrange for the location of the bribe or whether, his defense lawyer had created the defense after the fact. His perfidity well established, along with his fame, the Senator's reputation was set: He was dangerous, tricky, and hard to deal with in a county like Creek, where political corruption was a way of life. I could see M.C. beating both the contractor and Steve out of their money and told Steve I was more than a little worried.

"Don't sweat it, Hollywood. M.C. says he'll pay me and he'll pay me. The Senator may dance that contractor right out of court but I'll get my money. Just stay calm."

"Somehow, relying on the word of an ex-con with a slippery snake for a lawyer doesn't leave me real calm," I replied.

"You always were too serious. Let's go play golf and forget about it," Steve responded.

"I've got another case to work on Steve; I can't play golf today."

"See what I mean you're way too serious. I'm headed to the links—see you later."

* * * * *

The case once filed moved slowly, as justice often does in the rural courts of Oklahoma. A year later, Steve still didn't have his money nor had the case been tried, the Senator having gotten it postponed several times due to "legislative business." Monkey business would have been a more appropriate excuse. Then one Saturday morning another call came in—this one at home.

"Drop your socks and grab your jock, we're going to the cockfights!" Steve proclaimed.

"Hey, what if I can't go today, Steve," I replied.

"You've got to go; you're my lawyer. Today's the Big Meet and M.C.'s ready to pay off. We're goin' to Kellyville. Only tell your wife we've got a golf game in Tulsa. That's my cover. Be ready in an hour. I'll pick you up."

This time we headed out not in the old Town & Country but in Steve's new Lincoln. I told myself the cockfights might prove interesting and, to some extent, just getting there was. After leaving the highway and following a section-line road for several miles, Steve yanked the Lincoln onto an unmarked dirt road, which ran through ragged blackjack-covered hills too rough to farm. After some miles, we came to a gate guarded by an old man in a worn windbreaker. Steve flashed a card identifying himself as a member of good standing in the Gamebreeders Association. We paid an entrance fee and bumped our way across a dirt field to a large sheet-metal building.

Hopper met us at the door but said he was too busy to talk. He showed us to our seats in the bleachers and said he would see us later. The bleachers formed a square around the dirt cockpit, which was raised above the floor several feet. The pit itself was brightly lit; the arena, crowded, smoky, loud, and charged with the excitement of blood sport. For the most part, the spectators wore blue jeans and cowboy boots or work clothes. They looked like cowboys, farmers or ranchers, and blue-collar workers. Scattered through the crowd, however, were also gamblers and high-rollers with fists full of money and notebooks, furiously making and taking bets.

The fights went on continuously. Two handlers, one for each bird, would bring their roosters into the pit where a referee awaited. At his signal, the handlers released their birds. With no reluctance, the roosters hurled themselves at each other, slashing their opponent with gaffs, or knives, attached to their natural spurs. The fights were to the death, with each cock ever looking to inflict a mortal wound at best on the other or to cripple it by pecking out its eyes at worst. The birds struck with such speed that it was almost impossible to follow their attacks. Bred to fight, the roosters seemingly had the will to fight to the death. Even when down and mortally wounded, they pecked, scratched, and clawed their opponent until finally one or the other expired. It's hard to imagine an animal that has more fight in it, than a fighting cock.

Some people might find it bloody or inhumane but nothing about the cockfights bothered me. Are these birds any worse off than the steroid-injected chickens that live a few months in a packed barn with no natural light only to end up as the crispy special at KFC? In the world of crime, where does cockfighting rank? How does it possibly adversely affect society? Some would argue to their death against it, but I would counter that we have more serious things to worry about than two chickens fighting. It appeals, I always presumed, to those who enjoy watching boxing.

* * * * *

As I took in the action that night, Steve provided a running commentary on his rooster preferences:

"I like the Gray!" (Gray wasn't at all gray but blond.)

"The Red's more aggressive—lay a $100 on the Red."

"That one's from a breeder from Durant; he's best in the state."

And so it went for several hours, as the crowd ebbed and flowed and the gamblers and others cheered as the rooster of their choice finished its opponent off with a final strike or cursed as the neck of another was rung by a disappointed owner.

We spotted M.C. occasionally. Presiding over the meet, he moved through the crowd like a great ship, the people parting before him, like waves in the ocean. He would settle a dispute over a bet here, then deliver a message there, and next be seen giving advice to a handler or a referee elsewhere. He moved with surprising grace for such a big man, and I later learned that, in spite of his bulk, he had been the Missouri Valley tennis champion while at the University of Tulsa before going to prison. Finally, M.C. materialized before us and, beckoning with his hand, said, "Come on. It's payday."

We followed him beneath the stands to a corner of the building where he had set up a card table and some metal folding chairs as a makeshift office. Steve and I pulled up chairs as we watched M.C. pull out several bulging wads of bills from his worn denim pockets.

"Okay, partner it's time to settle up. I figure I owe you $17,000. Right, Steve?"

"How about interest and attorney fees," I piped up.

This started what lawyers like to call a lively discussion between M.C. and me, with M.C. using his fastest double-talk and Steve trying to get out of the way in case M.C. lost his temper and came after me. We finally settled on a round $18,200. Don't ask me how, but remember we're talking 1960 dollars.

"I'm ready to pay up but you all have to keep this absolutely quiet," M.C. decreed. "I do not want anyone—especially that contractor—to know I have money. That includes my lawyer; I don't trust him either. You can release the lien later when I tell you to."

"No problem!" Steve and I both quickly replied.

M.C. counted out the $18,200 in $100 and $1,000 bills. Yes, folks, we had $1,000 bills in those days. Then he pulled a pint of bourbon from his pocket and offered us a swig. Despite a mouth full of tobacco, he drank first; Steve and I both took a pull too.

After drinking on it, I told Steve I'd had about all the excitement I could stand for one day and he reluctantly agreed to leave. As we sailed down the turnpike headed for home, Steve looked at me and said: "Hollywood, I told you M.C. was good for it."

"I got to admit you were right, and I have to tell you that I was afraid I'd gone too far when I asked for fees and interest of $3,000," I replied.

"Yeah," Steve said. "Not only did I think M.C. might tear your head off but what you also didn't know is he's always packin'."

"Damn, Steve, thanks for telling me but a little late."

"Well, I figure you're the lawyer and you ought to be ready for anything. By the way, you're not really going to charge me a fee for all this fun are you?"

"Well, I'll take the $1,200—and that's just hush money for not telling Nancy where you really were today, and with that in mind, you also owe me a golf game at Southern Hills."

Steve laughed in reply: "Cheap at twice the price, Hollywood. The best thing about you is you've always got as much to hide as I do."

* * * * *

A few years later Steve was diagnosed with cancer.

He didn't last long.

What I didn't know that day at the Big Meet was that I had gained a new friend and sometime client: The wrongly convicted, vastly misunderstood M.C. Hopper. About every two or three years until his death, M.C. would burst into my office unannounced with some cockeyed legal problem that only he could scheme up and to his way of thinking, that only I could solve.

By the way, he always paid his bill, in cash.

THE DOC

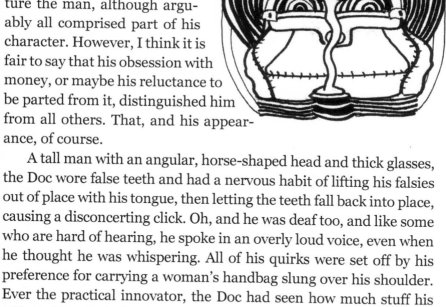

Skinflint is a good word. It isn't used much anymore, but it's the best word I can think of to describe the Doc.

Miserly, tight, frugal, or even greedy don't quite capture the man, although arguably all comprised part of his character. However, I think it is fair to say that his obsession with money, or maybe his reluctance to be parted from it, distinguished him from all others. That, and his appearance, of course.

A tall man with an angular, horse-shaped head and thick glasses, the Doc wore false teeth and had a nervous habit of lifting his falsies out of place with his tongue, then letting the teeth fall back into place, causing a disconcerting click. Oh, and he was deaf too, and like some who are hard of hearing, he spoke in an overly loud voice, even when he thought he was whispering. All of his quirks were set off by his preference for carrying a woman's handbag slung over his shoulder. Ever the practical innovator, the Doc had seen how much stuff his wife could carry in her purse and gotten one for himself.

The Doc became acquainted with me, because I was a friend of his son "Blinky" Bob, the nickname the result of a bad nervous blinking habit. Blinky was a few years older than my friends and me and became a hero to us younger boys, a reputation built upon his willingness to buy beer for us despite our being underage. Thus, I met the Doc, and years later when I began to practice law, he sought me out to act as his lawyer for what he deemed to be menial tasks.

I had no delusions as to why he chose me to represent him in such matters. He thought I would work cheap and saw nothing to dissuade him of this notion: I was young, just starting to practice law, a sole practitioner with a small, nondescript office in a nondescript building, and he'd had his fill of big law firms that had the audacity to charge a wealthy doctor a reasonable fee.

From my perspective, the Doc was a catch, a real live client who, despite bitching mightily about my invoices, paid his bills. Once early on in our attorney-client relationship while in my office, I had handed him a bill for several hundred dollars. He took one look at the bill, began gasping for breath, and staggered from my office as if having a heart attack. By that time, I knew him well and was not alarmed by the theatrics. When he returned, he solemnly stated: "I have taken care of entire families for a year for this much money."

I replied, "The bill is fair and you know it; pay it."

He did but begrudgingly. Later in reviewing these histrionics, I concluded Doc was testing me to see if I would compromise my bill. Had I reduced the fee that day, it would have indicated to him that I might also compromise a claim on his behalf. By sticking to the amount charged, I probably saved the Doc as a client, a mixed blessing for sure. As a legal client, he was hard to represent, opinionated, stubborn, and always sure he was right. He ignored most of my advice and usually acted according to his own counsel. On the other hand, he was always entertaining and had a sense of humor about almost everything else, save for when it came to money.

* * * * *

The Doc loved to conjure up get-rich-quick schemes and remained undaunted by failure. One of his first inventions that I recall was a portable irrigation system. Built out of thin wire, the entire system could be rolled on a spindle, hung on the back of a tractor, and then unrolled across a farmer's field. Holes were pierced in the metal strands, and when a source of water was attached to the apparatus, water dripped uniformly onto the field.

The Doc was overjoyed with his invention and sensed a fortune just waiting to be plucked from farmers who would see the wisdom in his device. But like even the best of products, the portable irrigation system needed marketing. So, the Doc drafted Blinky Bob and sent him off around the country to try to sell the system, driving a pickup with a prototype of the irrigation system attached.

When the Mosinee Paper Company bit on the idea, the Doc was ecstatic. He could already see the riches rolling in. But first, the Mosinee executives wanted a demonstration. No problem, the Doc owned several farms himself, one of which would make a great place to show off his beloved invention. A date was arranged, and the key decision-makers from Mosinee flew into Oklahoma City, where they were met by the Doc. With much fanfare, the businessmen were transported to the Doc's farm for the show-and-tell.

Blinky Bob was waiting at the farm to meet them, with the system attached to a tractor and ready for use. The executives, dressed formally in suits and clutching briefcases and notepads, lined up expectantly along the edge of the field. At the appointed moment, Blinky Bob floored the tractor and began to lay down the apparatus. The system unfolded as designed as it crossed the field, but Doc had failed to take into account the pesky Oklahoma wind.

It was April and the Doc should have known better. And, sure enough, in the middle of the demo, a mighty gust of wind picked up the entire metal irrigation system and carried it up into the air and over a neighboring field. The system was last seen headed north.

The Mosinee executives closed their briefcases and returned to their corporate offices in Yankeeland, pursued by none other than Doc, who tenaciously argued that such a slight design flaw could be remedied, but to no avail. To his credit, the Doc was undaunted by this setback, and soon launched a new invention, the no-splat frying pan. This contraption featured two frying pans welded together so that a pancake, an egg, sausage, or bacon could be flipped from pan to pan without splattering the cook. It is uncertain how many of these pans still exist, but I know I have never seen one anywhere but in the Doc's hands.

All of his inventions were grand, but the Doc's real love was real estate. He was a land hog, sucking up properties at every opportunity, relentlessly acquiring real estate in an attempt to become, at least in his mind, a land baron. As a young country doctor, he bought mineral rights in western Oklahoma and even took mineral rights as a fee from his patients. As his holdings increased, he parlayed this ownership into a thriving oil and gas business. When he moved to Oklahoma City, he turned his nimble mind again to real estate and acquired a large portfolio of cheap houses that he purchased for delinquent taxes, the bulk of which were located on Oklahoma City's predominately black, east side. If he was not a land baron, he was at least a slumlord.

And therein lies the tale.

The Doc owned a bar on Walnut Circle in the heart of a black neighborhood in the city. The bar was leased to one Bo Diddly Hurst, who initially operated his establishment at a profit and paid his rent, more or less, on time. But alas, Bo Diddly became a victim of Urban Renewal. The federal government, in its infinite wisdom, declared the neighborhood around the bar blighted, and the Urban Renewal Authority began to purchase or condemn the neighboring residences. As the project progressed, Bo Diddly's customers began to move out of the neighborhood, and the bar's business declined. As revenues fell, the rent began to go unpaid, and Bo Diddly fell further and further behind on the lease.

The Doc had a part-time employee who collected rents for him, but even this formidable collector could not squeeze a cent out of

Bo Diddly. Finally, as a last resort, the Doc came to me. My assignment: Evict Bo Diddly and sue him for back rents.

I pointed out that it might very well be difficult to collect anything from a failing bartender with no other means of support. However, since it would be necessary to go to court to obtain possession of the property, the Doc figured he might as well sue for the back rent while he was at it. Bo Diddly did not hire a lawyer, and was evicted and a judgment obtained against him for some $7,000 in rent, costs, and attorney fees.

After a judgment is entered, the judgment creditor has the right to summon the judgment debtor into court and examine the debtor under oath as to the nature and extent of his assets. Upon my examination of Bo Diddly's holdings, I found to my surprise that he owned two houses, his own home and a rent house. The homestead was exempt from execution under Oklahoma law, but the rent house was fair game, and although dilapidated, did represent an asset against which the Doc could attempt to enforce his judgment.

Before we could foreclose on the rental, however, Bo Diddly woke up. He hired a prominent black attorney, who was also a state senator, and based upon some dubious legal advise, Bo Diddly deeded the house to its occupant, his mother-in-law, the venerable Rosie Armstead. Bo Diddly then filed for personal bankruptcy, listing the Doc as his principal creditor.

Bankruptcy court was then, and remains now, a twilight zone where creditors can disappear into a black hole at the arbitrary whim of a precocious judge, and where intolerable delay is the rule, not the exception. After a few initial but inconclusive attempts to invalidate the deed in bankruptcy court, I filed a case on behalf of the Doc in Oklahoma District Court, asking the court to set aside the deed as an attempt to defraud creditors. Once again, we ran into multiple delays that dragged the case out and prevented a trial on its merits, as Bo Diddly's lawyer, the state senator, was entitled to continue, or pause, the case whenever the state legislature was in session, and he exercised his right to these legislative continuances mercilessly. Even when the legislature was not in session, Bo Diddly's lawyer managed to produce a long list of colorful grounds for continuances. He came just short of having his mother die twice. The continuances caused the Doc excessive heartburn, and gave me a cauliflower ear from the many telephone calls I got from the Doc haranguing me to get the job done and refusing to accept any explanation for further delay. Finally, even the Senator had run out of plausible excuses. The Judge's docket was cleared and the case was set for trial. In Oklahoma, the setting aside of a deed made to fraudulently avoid creditors is a matter which is tried before a judge and not a jury, so the case was in the hands of the trial judge, at his discretion.

The appointed day for the trial finally arrived. Doc and I were in court awaiting the Judge's entry. Bo Diddly and his lawyer were there too. The bailiff and the court reporter were present. Everything was set to finally dispose of the case. At the scheduled hour, the bailiff rose and intoned as usual, "All rise, hear ye, hear ye, the District Court of Oklahoma County is now in session, Honorable Charles Owens presiding." And the judge, Charles Owens, entered the courtroom from his chambers to take the bench.

As Doc stood, he leaned toward me as if to whisper in my ear, but instead, in his deaf man's thunderous roar, boomed out, "My God, you didn't tell me the judge was a n-----!"

It was truly life's darkest moment.

The bailiff heard it; the court reporter heard it; I heard it; Bo Diddly heard it; Bo Diddly's lawyer heard it; and yet to this day I don't know if Judge Owens heard it. He either didn't or he was certainly one of the world's most impartial judges, as after he heard all the evidence, which I must admit was overwhelmingly in the Doc's favor, Judge Owens set aside the deed, causing Bo Diddly's rent house to become available for the collection of Doc's judgment.

The story being about Doc, of course, it can't end here. Doc's insatiable quest for the almighty greenback would not be completed until he had captured Bo Diddly's property too. This was still not an easy given, as the setting aside of the deed only returned the property to Bo Diddly's bankruptcy estate. After due consideration to the legal niceties, however, the property was ordered sold for the benefit of creditors and notice was given of an auction date.

The sale was to be conducted by a U.S. Marshal at the house, where it would be sold to the highest bidder, with a minimum bid of two-thirds of the appraised value. The proceeds of the sale would then go into the bankruptcy, and since the Doc was by far the biggest creditor, he could bid on the property and actually recover a good part of the money he had paid for the property as a creditor.

As the day of the sale approached, the Doc grew increasingly nervous. His debt collector had heard a rumor that another notorious slumlord and buyer of cheap properties, "Bad Deed" Garrett, was going to bid on the property. This infuriated Doc, as he felt he had a proprietary interest in the house, even though he would have done the same thing to Bad Deed if the opportunity had arose.

The auction was set for 1:30 p.m. and the morning of the sale, Jerry O'Neal, a burly Irishman and the Deputy U.S. marshal who would conduct the bidding, called to ask if I had any special information about the sale. There was something about the whole situation that had me uneasy, and I suggested that he have at least two marshals present that afternoon. O'Neal thought this was overkill and pretty much scoffed at my suggestion, but ultimately did bring along another marshal with him.

Bo Diddly's rent house was in an area of Oklahoma City's east side that had yet to be touched by Urban Renewal. Set on a sleepy, tree-lined street, the modest one-story white frame home was perched on cinder blocks with a front porch bracketed by pillars that supported an overhanging roof. Since it was not air conditioned, the doors and screened windows of the house were open.

The Doc and I arrived about the same time as the marshals. The Doc was dressed in a tie and black suit, looking for all the world like an undertaker, or the villain from some old timey melodrama. Sure enough, Bad Deed Garrett was there too, along with several other individuals who looked like potential bidders, all clustered in the front yard under the hot Oklahoma sun.

The minute our little entourage began to ascend the front porch steps, however, things went off script. Rosie Armstead, a formidable, black woman surrounded by at least four of what appeared to be her grandchildren, stationed herself just inside the front screen door of the house and immediately challenged the marshals to identify themselves and their purpose. When told they were there to sell the house, Rosie shouted, "I'm calling my lawyer to keep you from selling my house!"

"Get off my property!" she demanded. Nothing the marshals said placated her. Instead, she stayed right where she was, occasionally screaming at the crowd, "You can't sell my house!"

The youngsters in the house followed her cue, and started yelling and screaming at the crowd too. With it clear that Rosie and company were not going to relent, Marshal O'Neal simply took a deep breath and began to read the Notice of Sale. In doing so, he failed to notice the gold Cadillac pulling up to the curb out front. The Caddy was one of those land yachts from the Sixties, meaning it measured at least six inches longer than any other car on the street, and was equipped with gold wire hubcaps and a vanity license plate that read "SONNY."

When the engine stopped, the door on the driver's side opened and the driver unfolded onto the pavement. He was the reincarnation of a young Jim Brown: Big, handsome, broad-shouldered, dressed in a tight-fitting golf shirt that displayed his massive chest and biceps. His expensive slacks and alligator loafers were set off by several gold chains around his neck. The newcomers began to saunter toward the house. Upon noticing the congregation of white men in suits gathered on the lawn, however, he turned his amble into a purposeful stride up the porch stairs to where Rosie waited.

"Sonny, they're selling my house! They can't sell my house I own it! I own it!"

Yep, Sonny looked to be just the kind of trouble I had been expecting to show up this day. His arrival had briefly paused the reading of the Notice of Sale by O'Neal, but now the marshal picked right back up where he had left off only to be confronted by a now glowering Sonny with his arms crossed over his chest.

"What's going on here?" Sonny said.

O'Neal replied, "We're U.S. Marshals, and we're selling this house under an order of the United States Bankruptcy Court."

Doc, ever curious and not wanting to miss anything, chose at this moment to lean in closer, while still supporting himself on one of the pillars. And then, all hell broke loose. Sonny knocked Doc's arm off the pillar, sending Doc reeling backward down the porch steps.

"Get your hands off my grandma's house!" Sonny yelled.

To which, Doc screamed, "I've been attacked! I've been attacked! Do something!" His false teeth and purse went flying. He stumbled into me, carrying both of us down the rest of the steps and into the front yard, where we struggled like two drunks trying to hold each other up. O'Neal grabbed Sonny from behind in a bear hug, as Sonny tried to toss the marshal off his back like a bronco at a rodeo. O'Neal was good-sized himself, another big man, but his feet left the ground as Sonny tried to heave him over his head. When O'Neal failed to heave, Sonny jammed an elbow into the marshal's side, but the tenacious O'Neal hung on. The other marshal then crossed the porch and kicked Sonny's feet out from under him. All three men crashed to the ground, landing in a big pile with the marshals on top and Marshal O'Neal still stuck to Sonny's back but now with a choke hold locked in place too. From the front door, Rosie screamed, "Let go of my grandbaby! Let go of my grandbaby!" as her grandchildren wailed behind her like a Greek chorus.

The two marshals finally managed to pull Sonny's arms back long enough to get handcuffs on his wrists. Doc and I got untangled, only to have Doc go right back down on his hands and knees to locate his teeth. As I watched him crawl across the yard, I couldn't help wondering how this would all end. I was pretty sure, not well.

Eventually, the two marshals got Sonny quieted down and escorted him to their car. O'Neal returned to reading the now crumpled Notice of Sale; the other marshal stayed with Sonny in the car. I looked around and realized that Bad Deed and the other potential bidders had disappeared. Rosie was still shouting and the children were still wailing, but somehow Marshal O'Neal persevered. A few minutes more, and he officially announced that the property was for sale to the highest bidder.

Undaunted, the Doc bid on the house and was declared highest bidder and the new owner.

I told Marshal O'Neal, I would take care of the paperwork with the court, and the Doc and I headed for my car. Suddenly, Doc grabbed me by the arm: "We've got to hurry and get to a phone!"

"What are you talking about?" I asked. "We've got to go get insurance before they burn it down."

"They'll burn the house down," he intoned.

With that, we hustled to a convenience store, found a pay phone, and I called my brother, an insurance agent, and had him put coverage on the house immediately. Nobody burned the house down, but later, it did take another trip to the house by the marshals to evict Rosie and her family, before Doc finally did get control of the property.

The next morning, Marshal O'Neal called me and thanked me for suggesting he bring help to the sale. In the end, they had simply let Sonny go with a stern warning, rather than filing any charges, as they were sympathetic to him and his grandmother and pretty much felt about Doc like most people who had to deal with him did.

So, yes, the Doc now owned the little house, which as it turned out, sat directly in the path of Urban Renewal, but what happened next is a story for another day.

CAT NAP

. . . .

Wern we were standing on the creek bank chucking rocks at turtles. We seldom hit the turtles, which was good for the turtles and really didn't bother us much. I was eleven and Barney, two months older, had just turned twelve. It was hot, but Oklahoma is always hot in August; although, somehow I remember it as being hotter in those days before air-conditioning.

"Your dad loves birds," Barney said.

"And he hates cats," I replied.

"Why's that?"

"They eat the birds."

Barney's throw almost clipped a big snapper, and with a splash, the turtle flopped into the muddy water. "How do you know he hates cats?"

"He shot one."

"You're lying."

"No, I saw it."

"Tell me about it."

So, here's the story I told.

My dad, dressed in a short-sleeve, white shirt and his suit pants, sat in our backyard on a hot summer evening. Day turned to dusk as he read the *Oklahoma City Times*, one of the nation's last evening newspapers. I was kicking a football up and down the yard, while the martins and swallows collected around our birdhouse, set on a pole some ten feet above the ground. You could hear the cicadas and only occasionally, a car passing by on the street. My dad's pride and joy, a black '48 Cadillac convertible, was parked in the driveway, like a movie scene from the Fifties, repeated house by house in our middle-class suburban neighborhood. Into this tranquil setting crept a cat. He came stealthily through our flower bed, headed for the birdhouse. At first my dad didn't see the cat, but when he did, Dad stiffened, the newspaper came down, and his guard went up. Our visitor looked like any ole ordinary gray cat to me but to my dad he was clearly the enemy.

"That cat's after our birds," Dad said.

"I'll run him off," I said, cocking my arm to wing the football at the feline intruder.

"No, he'll come back when we're not here. Go in the house and get my shotgun."

"But Dad, that's someone's cat."

"No, he's a stray cat, I can tell. Besides, he shouldn't be in our yard anyway. Get my shotgun."

In our family, my dad was not a person you refused, and even though the cat looked well fed, clean, and like he belonged to someone, I went into the house and returned with the shotgun. It was a double barrel 12 gauge Remington that Dad used for turkey hunting, favoring a 20 gauge pump for quail. I handed my dad the gun and a box of shells. Having never suffered from indecision, Dad promptly loaded the gun and then rose from his chair, aimed, and fired. The cat virtually disintegrated before my eyes, turning one moment from cat to the next into a shapeless mass of bloody fur.

Dad calmly handed me the gun back and said, "Take the gun in the house and clean up the cat." He then resumed reading his newspaper as if nothing had happened.

Using a shovel and a garbage bag, I scraped up what was left of the kitty and gave him a proper burial in one of our garbage cans. A day or two later, I answered the door and found Cynthia waiting. She was a girl who went to my school and lived down the street.

"Have you seen my cat?" she said.

"No," I replied instantly, "but, I'll keep an eye out for him."

At this point in my story, Barney interrupted to announce, "I've seen her tits."

"She barely has any, and I don't believe it."

"She showed them to me."

"Horse manure."

"Look at the snake!" Barney yelled, and as I jerked my head around to look, he tripped me and pushed me over backward, laughing all the while.

On our way home, Barney said, "Your dad hates cats."

"No, he loves birds."

OLD MAN WHITNEY

· · · · · · · · · · · ·

No one had ever heard of Post-traumatic Stress Disorder in 1952. Back then, consulting a psychiatrist meant a person was crazy, and most Americans shared General Patton's view that soldiers who couldn't fight for mental reasons were simply cowards.

We had, however, heard of being shell-shocked, and Mr. Whitney was for sure that. He had been a naval gunnery officer on a cruiser in the Pacific that provided cover for the attacks on Iwo Jima and Okinawa. The U.S. Navy bombarded the Japanese for days at a time, while fighting off Kamikaze attacks.

The effect of the exposure to the constant roar of the big Navy guns was obvious in Mr. Whitney: He chain smoked. He jerked. He twitched. He squirmed, and he couldn't sit still, always lurching around the classroom, sitting on his desk, or pacing nervously. Sometimes, he'd scratch himself as if bugs were crawling all over him.

The effect of the exposure to the constant roar of the big Navy guns was obvious in Mr. Whitney.

He was from Back East somewhere, a graduate of Yale, who spoke with a refined accent, far smoother than the southwestern twang to which we were accustomed. Why he chose to teach at a small school in Oklahoma, no one knew. Later, I guessed that it was probably to avoid the pressures of a job on Wall Street or other big city life. In any event, he was a Yankee, a term that my older brother, who I idolized, used mainly as an insult.

Mr. Whitney's job was to try to teach American history to a room full of disinterested twelve-year-olds, possessed of at least an ordinary amount of childish cruelty. However, once we knew he was vulnerable, we harassed him relentlessly. When his back was turned to write on the blackboard, we dropped books or slammed down the windows. Any loud noise could make him jump, much to our delight. My friend Bill was believed to have achieved the ultimate irritation by dropping a pocketful of change on the floor. Mr. Whitney might have been a little deaf but he sure heard that.

To his credit, Mr. Whitney never lost his cool—despite our antics. Of course, he knew what was happening in his classroom, but he pressed on with his teaching, and as I'm sure he had calculated, we gradually became bored with our own tricks and stopped bothering him. Ironically, he was an interesting teacher, and we all learned something from him in spite of ourselves and, in my case, even developed a lifelong interest in American History.

I heard later that he died fairly young of Parkinson's disease, maybe caused by his shot nerves but who knows. Once I left his classroom to move on to the eighth grade, I hardly ever thought of Mr. Whitney again, until the other day. I was sitting in an airport bar and the waitress dropped a tray of glasses. The young soldier next to me jumped and ducked like he'd been shot.

In that moment, I was reminded of Old Man Whitney. He wasn't even thirty years old in 1952.

FLOYD'S TROUBLE

. . . .

Floyd hit the Deputy with a tire chain, an overhead blow that caught the Deputy across the neck and shoulder driving him to his knees. The Deputy still got his gun out, but then Floyd hit him again, backhanding him in the head and face, knocking him senseless.

Trouble was nothing new to Floyd. If he didn't find it, then it found him. He had just done three years in the Missouri State Penn for a Saint Louis payroll job. The job itself had gone well. Floyd and Pat had charged into the store with guns drawn and grabbed the cash just after it was taken off of the armored truck. Pat's friend Ernie helped carry the money and drove the car. Floyd had never seen Ernie before but trusted Pat. That was his mistake. Ernie bought a brand new Pontiac and drove it around town. He hit all the bars and drank too much and talked too much. When the cops picked Ernie up, he spilled his guts. Floyd and Pat were grabbed before they even had time to think about running.

Floyd vowed to himself:
No more jobs with someone he couldn't trust.

After Floyd had gotten out of jail this last time, he went to stay with his brother in the Cookson Hills while he figured out what to do. Being an ex-con, he wasn't likely to get a job, even if there was one to

49

be had. His best bet was still to rob banks, but he knew he'd have to play it smarter—hook up with pros and make some big scores. Floyd vowed to himself: No more jobs with someone he couldn't trust.

He had location going for him. Part of the old Cherokee Nation, the rugged, remote Cookson Hills were made to avoid the law. The people were clannish and hated the government. Nearly all poor, they considered robbing from banks just a way to get by and get even. As for Floyd, well, while he weighed his options, he hunkered down in a cabin back in the hills, and, with his brother, roamed the woods, hunting, fishing, and drinking shine. After a couple of weeks, Floyd was bored and running out of money. He decided to go into Sallisaw and see Ginny, and then, move on to Kansas City where he could hookup with a prison friend and get back to his chosen profession.

Ginny lived outside of town in a little, rundown house on a few acres of poor farmland that gave up just enough for her to scratch out a living. About ten years older than Floyd, Ginny had once been married but the worthless husband was long gone, having left her with a baby girl, some chickens, and a few hogs. Dusk had fallen as Floyd drove down the rutted dirt road to Ginny's house. He pulled up in front and honked. Ginny came out on the porch barefoot, wearing a thin cotton dress. There was still enough light that Floyd could see she had nothing on underneath. Nearly good-looking, Ginny had the hands of someone used to hard work and a face lined by too many days in the hot sun, but her body was still slim and she stood up straight and strong in the Oklahoma twilight.

"Hello, Charlie. I heard you was out of jail. I hoped you'd come see me," she said.

"I missed you, Ginny," Floyd replied.

"Come on in and I'll put the baby to bed."

"Got any shine?" Floyd asked as he stepped up the front steps.

"Shit, Charlie, I've always got shine. I may be poor but around here, somebody will always have some shine to share. Hell, you should know that." Floyd laughed and said, "Well then, pour us one and let's party." And party, they did, drinking and making love most of the night while the baby slept in the other room.

The next day, Ginny was up early by habit, but Floyd laid around in bed until long after sunup. Later in the day, they headed into town to get a meal at the local hotel. That's where the trouble started. Floyd had no more parked his car and he and Ginny started toward the hotel, when Floyd saw the Deputy whipping a mule.

The mule, a sorry-looking animal so skinny his ribs showed like Braille, stood in the middle of the street, hitched to a farmer's wagon. The wagon was blocking traffic and the mule wouldn't budge. The Deputy had grabbed the farmer's bullwhip and was thrashing the mule when the scene caught Floyd's eye. Floyd noticed that not only would the mule not budge, but the animal appeared to dig its hooves in even harder with every lash of the whip.

The day was hot, and the Deputy was sweating and cussing. Floyd watched as he whipped the mule harder and harder. Always a bully, the Deputy was a big, pig-eyed man, and he and Floyd had a history. The Deputy had arrested Floyd on a chicken-shit charge of stealing a hog. The charge didn't stick but there'd been bad blood between the two men ever since.

Without even thinking, Floyd stepped into the street and yelled at the Deputy. "Stop beating that mule, you dumb asshole."

"Ain't none of your damn business, Pretty Boy!" said the Deputy.

"I told you to never call me that, you worthless piece of shit," Floyd said.

The Deputy didn't bother to look up, just kept beating the mule.

Floyd walked back to his car, opened the trunk, and pulled out a tire chain.

"I'm going to whip your ass," Floyd said.

"Like hell, you are!" the Deputy said, as Floyd strode toward him.

The Deputy went for his gun and that's when Floyd hit him. The Deputy went down, bloodied, his jaw obviously broken.

As for Floyd, well, he was on the run again, his natural state.

UNCLE EARL

· · · · · · · · · · · ·

My brother and I never really liked Christmas, except for Uncle Earl. I think our dad felt the same way but he would never say so because Mom liked Christmas. She always put up a tree and we all had to decorate it with her. This was supposed to be a big deal but it only mattered to Mom. I did, however, find it fun to throw the fake snow on the tree. I don't know if I ever told her that. We got presents but being pretty well-off that wasn't such a big deal either since we already had toys and clothes and even bikes.

This all changed the day Uncle Earl came to Christmas dinner.

He had been living out west somewhere—Arizona, I think—and had recently moved back to town. I was ten or eleven that year and I had never seen this uncle before. It's hard to forget that first Christmas with him. The doorbell rang: I answered; and there was Earl. Before I said anything, he yelled out: "Christmas gift!" Followed by, "I got you, Kid. I said it first. You owe me one good joke." Then he jumped up in the air and did a little dance. I'd never before seen anything like that—or anyone, for that matter.

The doorbell rang, I answered, and there was Earl. . . . Then he jumped up in the air and did a little dance.

Uncle Earl was a big man, over six feet tall and overweight but not gone to fat. He had the florid face of a drinker and wore a cheap suit and a tie. Whatever else one could say about him, he damn sure liked to have a good time. That first Christmas with him, right after his Christmas greeting and the dance, he shot out his hand to me and said, "Put'er there; which one are you?" I

53

told him my name but it didn't really matter, as all he ever called anybody was "Pard" or "Babe" or "Honey." The only exceptions to this were my mom and dad. I could tell he respected my mom because he always called her by her name. He called my dad, Sonny Boy.

Names exchanged, he danced his way into the house, yelling out, "Earl's here—let the party begin!" He grabbed my mom and gave her a big hug, something my dad didn't even do very often. Then he did a complete pirouette, snatched my brother off of the floor, and swung him through the air in a big circle like an airplane.

Dad said, "Earl, where the hell have you been?"

Uncle Earl replied "Now, Sonny Boy, you know that's none of your damn business." Then he pulled a bottle of whiskey out of a brown sack he was carrying in his suit pocket and said, "I brought my good friend Jack Daniels. Get us some glasses!"

Dad got some glasses and Earl poured them each a big shot of whiskey. He raised his glass in a toast and said, "Merry Christmas, a Happy New Year, prosperity, and pussy" and swallowed a big gulp.

My mom said, "Now, Earl, you watch your language."

To my surprise, Uncle Earl replied, "I'll watch my language when someone watches me." With that, he downed another big gulp.

And to my greater surprise, my mom said not another word.

He then declared: "I brought these boys a fine present."

With that, he reached in his pocket and pulled out a somewhat scuffed baseball. He held it aloft and said, "This baseball was hit out of Texas League Park by none other than Al Rosen, who went on to play for the Cleveland Indians and was a great third baseman and a dynamite hitter. They called Al: 'The Hebrew Hammer.' I picked it up at the place I worked, which sat just over the left-field fence at the ballpark. Al was in the minor leagues, at the time, on his way up. It's for you boys."

And he tossed the baseball to me.

The Al Rosen baseball was the best Christmas present I had ever gotten. I was dumbfounded. Mom said, "What do you say?"

I was so shocked that I just looked at her and said, "What?"

"Remember your manners. Thank, Uncle Earl."

"Oh, thanks, Uncle Earl, this is great," I said.

"Okay, Pard. In a few years, you'll hit it out of the park."

I never did but I still have that baseball.

* * * * *

After the gift bestowing, Uncle Earl, of course, kept on drinking, and a few minutes later, my mother's sister, Jane, arrived. If the world ever made two incompatible people, it was Earl and Jane. The difference was that Uncle Earl didn't know they were incompatible, didn't care they were incompatible, or both. As for Aunt Jane, well, she was a caricature of the uptight older, single woman. Back then, she probably would have been called a "spinster" or an "old maid." She'd never met Uncle Earl before and the pleasure was definitely not hers. When they were introduced, Earl slapped her on the ass and said, "Baby, how about a drink." It wasn't a question.

Jane was so flabbergasted by this that she didn't manage to speak before Earl had put a big shot of whiskey in her hand and roared out: "Jane missed our first toast, so here's to Santa Claus and all of his little midgets."

Jane, who by now had recovered, corrected him: "Those are elves and I don't drink."

"Elves, midgets, who cares, the point is the drink not the toast. But if you don't drink it, don't waste it," he said, as he grabbed Jane's drink and threw it back himself.

"I believe I'll help fix dinner," Jane said.

"Jane, I don't really need any help. I started early and I'm almost ready," Mom replied.

"No! No! I insist!" And with that, Aunt Jane fled—some would say, retreated—to the kitchen, away from Uncle Earl who seemed determined to refuse to recognize that there was a war of the sexes going on in our living room.

* * * * *

Before Uncle Earl, the best thing about Christmas was dinner. We always had the same thing: turkey, dressing, mashed potatoes, and cranberries. Dessert was always pecan pie. My brother and I weren't allowed to eat sweets very often but at Christmas, we had our piece of pie and could even have ice cream on top.

With Uncle Earl, Christmas dinner was more, well, profane. As Dad carved the turkey, my father went around the table one by one, asking each of us if we preferred white or dark meat. When it was Earl's turn to choose, my uncle replied, "Give me the dark meat, Sonny Boy. A man's not a man until he's tasted dark meat."

I tried not to laugh and knew better than to look at my brother who was overcome with the same problem. Aunt Jane sat up like she'd been poked with a cattle prod. "Would you please refrain from anymore vulgar remarks," she said.

"Lighten up, Baby. It's a holiday," Earl said.

Dad quickly turned the conversation to horses, which the two brothers both loved. My dad liked everything about horses, including riding them. Uncle Earl was more interested in betting on them and my dad liked to do that too, so they were soon arguing the relative merits of last year's Kentucky Derby and Preakness winners.

Meanwhile, Uncle Earl went after his food like he hadn't eaten in weeks. When his mouth was full, which was the only thing that shut him up, my brother, who was a lot bolder than me, asked, "Dad says you were in the war. What did you do?"

Uncle Earl swallowed and replied, "Pard, I was a Seabee. Do you know what that is?"

"I saw a movie with John Wayne; he was a Seabee."

"John Wayne was a draft dodger. All that brave stuff he does in movies is just for show," Uncle Earl said.

"Were you in the South Pacific?" my brother asked.

"Yes, I was, and it's damn sure not what it's cracked up to be in that play that's so popular. In fact, it's hot, humid, and overrun with mosquitoes. Those Polynesian women aren't much either. Most of them are fat and have the clap. The boys who went with 'em couldn't pass short-arm inspection."

Confused, my brother said: "I thought Seabees built stuff but Dad said you fought the Japs."

"Pard, I don't talk about that. It was your dad who really helped win the war."

"What do you mean?"

"We enlisted at the same time. There were maybe a couple of hundred guys like us signing up. Everybody had to pass a physical, and then they gave us some kind of IQ test. We were all sitting around and waiting for them to tell us whether we got in or not and a Captain comes out and calls Sonny Boy's name. The Captain took your father away and I didn't see him again until the war was over."

"What happened?" my brother said.

"Your dad scored so high on that IQ test, they took him and made him a spy."

"Like a real spy? Like James Bond?" my brother asked. "He just told us he was in the Navy, moved around the South Pacific, and never saw combat."

"Well, technically, that's probably true, but who knows? He still won't tell anybody what he did. Me, I think he broke the Japanese code. Anyway, he learned to speak Japanese. Didn't you, Sonny Boy?"

"Earl," my father said quietly, "we aren't going to talk about that. I was lucky I never got shot at like you did."

57

With that, Earl raised his glass and proclaimed, "Here's to all those slanty-eyed, little bastards who couldn't shoot straight." My dad laughed but turned the conversation to the big, new building they were constructing downtown, something in which our whole family was interested.

After we finished dinner, Aunt Jane hopped up to help my mother clear the table, and Uncle Earl announced that he better be leaving because he had a date with "a young lovely." To which my father replied, "I've seen some of your dates, Earl, and there wasn't anything lovely about any of them."

"Of course, compared to what you have, Sonny, that's true. She's good looking and she can cook too," Earl said as he hugged my mom and started for the door. He hadn't gotten far when looked back at Jane and said, "Good to meet you, Hon." His words were met by a cold stare. Jane said nothing. After Uncle Earl left, my brother and I turned our attention to pestering Dad to tell us what he and Earl had done in the war. Dad never would say what he had done but did finally admit he was in U.S. Naval intelligence.

As for Uncle Earl, his war story was quite a tale.

As Earl had said, he was a Seabee, a name Dad told us derived from the initials C.B. for Construction Battalion, a piece of trivia I remember to this day. The Seabees built airfields and other installations, and Uncle Earl's job was driving a bulldozer. Although not a fighting outfit per se, the Seabees were trained to shoot and Earl carried a big .45 Colt. It turned out that was a good thing.

His unit went ashore at Guadalcanal right behind the attacking forces, and within a few days, they had moved inland and started to clear out the jungle and rebuild the Japanese airstrip there. Uncle Earl was working with a squad of eight men bulldozing trees around the perimeter of the base, when the Japanese counterattacked. Before the U.S. Marines, who were protecting them, could get there, four of the Seabees were killed and all of the others wounded. Earl killed at least three Japanese soldiers with his .45. Another Japanese bayoneted Uncle Earl in the side before Earl took the man's rifle away from him and beat him to death with his own gun. Earl nearly bled to death from his injuries and was awarded a Purple Heart and some other citations. He also got sent back to Hawaii for the rest of the war. Just like at dinner, Uncle Earl would never talk about the battle, and my dad told us he only knew the details because his job let him read Earl's records.

I had only just met Uncle Earl, but I already liked him and treasured my baseball. However, when I learned what he had done in WWII, he became my first real life hero. Unfortunately, I picked up a few of my uncle's habits other than bravery as well, but at least I got a little of his sense of humor. When Christmas came around the next year, the first thing I asked was whether Uncle Earl was coming to dinner. Mom said that was a bit of a problem as Jane didn't want to come if Earl did.

Without thinking, I blurted out: "Well, don't ask Jane!"

Mom said, "They are both family, and it's not right to leave either one out. I'll talk to Jane and I'm sure we can work it out."

Mom was good at talking to people and sure enough, she convinced Aunt Jane to come to dinner even though Uncle Earl was going to be there too. This time I stood watch for Earl, and when I threw the door open to meet him, I yelled "Christmas gift!"

"You got me, Pard. I owe you a present, but I don't know what it will be. Maybe I can find something," he said, as he rummaged through his pockets. After a spell, he said, "I'm sorry. I can't find anything. I may have to give you an IOU."

Before disappoint could set in, however, he suddenly said, "Oh no, here's something, but I'm not sure you'll care anything about it." With that, he pulled out a bone-handled pocketknife and handed it to me. It turned out he had one for my brother as well.

Uncle Earl had also brought a bottle of French champagne, which he opened saying, "The French can't fight a lick, but they damn sure know how to make love and champagne." Mom brought out three glasses but Earl protested, "These boys need a glass! In France, everybody drinks wine." After a mild protest, Mom said, okay, and gave my brother and me champagne glasses, but she told Earl, "Just a little bit for the boys."

If Earl hadn't already been my hero, giving me champagne would have elevated him to hero status. My brother and I had snuck a few beers from the icebox but other than that, I had never had a drink before. To this day, I consider champagne a special drink for special occasions, and I'm sure it will never taste quite as good as that first taste did that Christmas day.

* * * * *

The talk at dinner that year was all about football, or more specifically, the Oklahoma Sooners, coached by Bud Wilkinson. Wilkinson had one of his best teams and O.U. was headed to the Orange Bowl to play Alabama. Dad was a Sooner fan but Uncle Earl was convinced Alabama would win the game. The brothers argued about this over dinner until they finally ended up betting fifty dollars on the outcome.

I realized watching them that I had learned something else from Uncle Earl's visits—mainly that you can argue like hell and not get mad and even still be friends when it's over. Earl and Dad seemed to argue about almost everything but they never really got mad at each other. Up until then, most of the arguments I'd ever had had ended in playground fights or hurt feelings; now I realized that was mostly stupid and definitely unnecessary.

At dinner, my brother had some new questions for our uncle: "What kind of work do you do?"

"I'm a salesman, Pard. I can sell ice boxes to Eskimos."

"What are you selling now?" my brother asked.

"I'm glad you asked," Uncle Earl said. "Most of time, I'm selling cancer insurance policies but I came up with a product that's going to make me rich: inflatable dolls. Not the kind that sailors take on long sea trips, no sir. These babies are for practicing CPR. You know what that is, Pard?"

"I think so. It's when you try to save people with heart attacks?"

"Not just heart attacks but drownings, strokes, smoke inhalation, all kinds of emergencies. My customers are fire departments, police forces, schools—anywhere they teach CPR. It can't miss!" Uncle Earl said.

"Damn, Earl, that sounds like another one of your crackpot schemes," Dad said.

"Only crackpot to you. If you're goin' to make big money, you've got to take a chance, Sonny Boy," Earl said.

"Well, all I can remember is your donut shops that only opened for dinner and your mink farm scheme," Dad replied.

"Now, Sonny, not every deal's a winner, but this one is. I can feel it," said Earl.

After dinner, Uncle Earl took my brother and me and our new knives out in the yard and showed us how to throw them so they stuck in the ground as well as in trees or our wooden fence. We must have learned a little bit that day from Uncle Earl's training as neither one of us ever cut ourselves or any of our friends. My brother actually practiced enough that he could throw his knife pretty hard and hit a target, practicing being another way to avoid homework.

After that second Christmas, I only saw Uncle Earl a couple of times again. He came by to pick up his bet when Alabama beat O.U. in the Sugar Bowl. Joe Namath had thrown a touchdown pass and Leroy Jordan made thirty-one tackles all by himself, one of the greatest defensive performances of all time. Uncle Earl was his usual self that day, and when he collected the money from Dad, he did so while yelling, "Roll Tide" and waving his fist in the air.

The next time he came over to our house, Earl didn't look so good. He seemed worried and didn't have any jokes to tell. He and Dad went outside to talk privately but left the door open. I tried to hear what they were talking about. If I heard them right, it sounded like Earl was broke and needed a loan. Dad lectured him about his crazy schemes but after they talked, they went into Dad's study and I think Dad wrote Earl a check.

When Christmas came around again, the first thing I wanted to know was if Uncle Earl would be there. Mom said he'd moved away again; this time, she thought, to Florida. Of course, Aunt Jane came. She had nowhere else to go. The dinner part of Thanksgiving was still good but without Uncle Earl, a lot of the fun was gone. My folks seemed to miss him too, and they made an effort to try and make things fun, even taking us to the movies. But it wasn't the same.

I didn't think about Uncle Earl too much after that until the day the phone rang one weekend. Mom answered it and immediately called Dad to come talk. Right off, by the way my dad's face looked as he listened on the call, I could tell something was wrong. When he set the phone down, he said, "My god, Earl's dead." Then, for the first, last, and only time, I saw my dad cry. It shocked me. He was the toughest guy I knew and he never showed emotion.

Mom told me to go outside and leave them alone but she didn't need to, I felt so uncomfortable I just wanted out of there. It was strange. I felt bad about Uncle Earl and I felt bad for Dad but mostly I was shook up from seeing my dad cry.

A little later, he came outside and put his arm around me and said, "I know how much you liked Earl, but it will be okay." It was confusing. Usually Dad was the one who cheered me up when something was wrong but this time I felt like I was supposed to cheer him up. I couldn't think of anything to say, however, so I ended up not saying anything. After a while, Dad went back in the house to make plans to go take care of Earl's body.

It was awhile before the world seemed quite right again.

Now I've got nephews myself and when I see them, I try to make them feel good like Uncle Earl did for me. It works a little but I just don't have Earl's style, though I do still have that baseball.

A LITTLE MISUNDERSTANDING

. . . .

"**L**isten, you little pissant, you better keep your damn mouth shut." Sheriff Ed Lang was mad. It didn't happen often but some could still remember him at fifteen grabbing a shovel and beating the crap out of the Dobbs boys. The two of them were seventeen and eighteen, grown men really, but they bullied Ed one too many times. His fury on this day was aimed at Franz Schroeder, an attorney in the wrong place, on the wrong job.

With his black, slicked-down hair and narrow, thin-lipped face, Schroeder was the proverbial Yankee to the sheriff's beloved local boy. Schroeder didn't help his own case any either, given that he tended to talk in a perpetual snarl and was suspicious of everyone. On this particular day, however, their conflict was a matter of happenstance. *Is it true* The attorney had picked up the job that had *Schroeder has* Sheriff Ed so mad almost by accident when his *taken to* predecessor died unexpectedly and the county *wearing a* suddenly needed a county attorney to cover the *metal vest?* criminal docket.

It was a mismatch from the start—not only was Sheriff Ed a local boy but he was also a veteran, a veteran of World War I no less. A tall, rangy man, always dressed in a cowboy hat and boots, Sheriff Ed had grown up on a farm south of Madill near the Red River. He had come back home from WWI a sergeant, with a Purple Heart and a limp that was permanent.

He was all the law there was in a lawless county made even more so by the passage of prohibition.

At issue between the two men on this day was a subpoena Schroeder had issued for a witness in a case against a local bootlegger. The sheriff's deputies had been unable to find the witness, and when Sheriff Ed informed Schroeder, the county attorney had implied that the sheriff was on the take from said bootlegger. It was the kind of insulting remark he routinely made to Sheriff Ed, and he had then made matters worse by following it up with a directive: "Well, why don't you go back and look a little harder," he said.

"Don't tell me how to do my job. My deputies know this county and everyone in it. If they couldn't find him, he ain't there."

"I'll see if the judge will appoint a special deputy to serve the summons. Someone who doesn't 'know everybody in the county,' " Schroeder replied.

"As far as I'm concerned, you can wipe your ass with that subpoena—just don't waste your time bothering me about it again," said Sheriff Ed.

Schroeder started to say something else, but thinking better of it, instead turned and walked into the courthouse.

* * * * *

Across the street at the local café, Earl and Bobby Jack were drinking coffee as they watched the sheriff stalk off.

"Them two just can't get along," said Earl. Earl was a local farmer and his cousin Bobby Jack ran the feed and seed store.

"Nobody could get along with Franz. The county commissioners ought to run his ass off. He's no damn good," Bobby Jack said.

"They probably would if they could find any other lawyer who wanted the job," said Earl.

"Hell, aren't but two more in the county and one's rich and don't want the job and the other's a damn drunk," said Bobby Jack.

"We better find out where he's getting his whiskey. The way these damn revenuers are shutting down the bootleggers, it's soon going to be hard to find a drink around here," Earl said.

"What's wrong with people? The government doesn't even want an honest man to have a drink," Bobby Jack said woefully.

"You know them damn preachers are the biggest drinkers there is. By the way, here comes Schroeder now," Earl said.

"Why's he walking so all bent over like that, he looks like he's pushing into a tornado," Bobby Jack said.

"You didn't hear?" Earl said. "He's wearing a metal vest he had made under his shirt. Probably weighs at least twenty pounds. He says he wears it case anyone wants to take a shot at him. He looks like a damn fool."

"I can't believe he's that afraid of the sheriff."

"I wouldn't want to have the sheriff on my ass," Earl said. "That son of a bitch is tough."

"It's just bullshit," Bobby Jack said, looking insulted on the sheriff's behalf. "Sheriff Ed never shot anyone but that one guy, and he come at him with a knife."

"How about the war? I bet he killed plenty of them Krauts."

"That ain't the same," Bobby Jack said. "Anyway, I got to get back to work. I'll flip you for the coffee."

"Only if we use my coin. You've probably got one of those two-headed ones like they have at the fair."

"Screw you," said Bobby Jack. "We'll just arm wrestle for it."

"Shut up and flip."

Earl lost the toss and called the waitress over so he could pay.

Schroeder came into the café right after the ticket had been settled. He looked at the two men but did not say hello and took a seat at the counter by himself."

"Squirrel," Earl said.

"You got that right," Bobby Jack replied.

* * * * *

The sheriff pulled his beat-up, Model T Ford into his driveway. He lived in a modest, red brick house on the edge of town. His wife kept a vegetable garden in the backyard, which ran down the hill into a wooded area. The sheriff had built a fence around the garden to try and keep out the rabbits and the deer after both one summer had taken to using the garden as a regular dining spot.

He entered the house and threw his cowboy hat on the table. "I need a good drink of that illegal whiskey," he muttered to himself. He found his wife, Maggie, in the kitchen, fixing dinner. Maggie was a tall woman, half Apache, neither plain nor pretty. The two of them had met in Lawton when he was mustering out of the service at Fort Sill. They married right away, and she took a job teaching at the local grade school. They'd had no children but got along well enough.

"See the sheriff is breaking the law again," Maggie said.

"Only in the sanctity of my own home."

"Maybe I should turn you in to the county attorney. I'm sure he'd love to get something on you."

"You did have to mention him. He's why I need a drink."

The sheriff took a water glass and a bottle of bourbon out of the cabinet, set down at the kitchen table, and poured himself a stiff shot. Maggie got herself a glass and joined him.

"Don't mind if I do," she said, extending her glass.

Ed poured her a drink and said, "I hear it's dangerous to get an Indian drunk."

"Contrary to public opinion, we can hold our firewater, particularly if it's the good stuff. So what did your favorite public servant do today?"

"I ought to twist his head off and feed it to the hogs. The little prick accused me of being on the take from some bootlegger."

"Not Uncle Bob I hope?" Maggie said.

"No, Uncle Bob had the good sense to put his still over in Carter County after he and I had a little talk."

"Is it true Schroeder has taken to wearing a metal vest? I heard that today from one of the parents at school."

"Yeah, it's true, what an idiot."

"Ed, now seriously, you be careful with that guy. Anyone who is paranoid enough to have a metal vest made and wear it, is crazy enough to do something stranger still," Maggie cautioned him.

"Spoken like a true school teacher. Think I'll have just one more small drink."

* * * * *

For a few days, the sheriff went about his regular business with nary a thought of the county attorney. For months, he'd been trying to catch some small-time cattle rustlers. The thieves worked at night and were surprisingly restrained, singling out one or two cows at a time, slaughtering and butchering them on the spot—taking only the best cuts of beef.

There were a lot of rumors about the identity of the rustlers but no real clues. Sheriff Ed was working a new lead from a local gas station attendant who had overhead two customers talking about a guy across the river in Texas who sold prime beef at cut-rate prices. When one of the men asked how the seller did it, the other just laughed and said, "You'll have to ask Elmer." This conversation had been relayed to a sheriff's deputy, who relayed it to Sheriff Ed, and the hunt for Elmer was on. By coincidence, Ed's deputy had an uncle who happened to live in Denison, and when the deputy called him to ask if he knew anyone named Elmer in town, the uncle immediately said, "That's got to be Elmer Stone. He's crooked as a snake, always has some kind of shady deal working."

With the cooperation of a Texas sheriff, Sheriff Ed had Stone brought in for questioning. Being no neophyte to the ways of the law, Stone demanded a lawyer. Eventually, after some negotiation, Stone agreed to give up the names of the two Oklahomans who had sold him beef in exchange for an agreement not to prosecute him.

The local rustlers turned out to be a couple of no-good, white trash crooks with lengthy criminal records, who lived near the town of Kingston: Earl Fain and Bob Garlock. The question then was, how to catch them in the act. A little more persuasion, and Stone agreed to tell the rustlers he needed more beef, right away. Sheriff Ed ordered his deputies to keep an eye on the rustlers.

The county owned four cars. Sheriff Ed had one as did each of the three county commissioners. The sheriff borrowed one of those for his deputies to use for the surveillance and set up his operation at the general store in Kingston, only three miles from where the rustlers were holed up. It wasn't hard to watch the rustlers' place without being seen. They lived in a rundown wooden shack up a rough trail, off of a dirt farm road. Between the road and the house was a thick stand of blackjack trees. The deputies could park on the road and not be seen from the rustlers' shack. If the deputies wanted or needed a closer look, they could approach the shack on foot through the trees without being detected.

In the end, it didn't take long for Fain and Garlock to make a move. The day after getting the order from Stone, just before dusk, they started packing up their wagon with lanterns, a .22 rifle, and knives and saws for butchering. One of the deputies rushed to Kingston to alert Sheriff Ed, while the other one stayed behind to keep an eye on Fain and Garlock. As darkness fell, the rustlers emerged and began to hitch up their mules to the wagon. Since they had to be back before daylight, they couldn't go too far; Fain and Garlock weren't exactly criminal geniuses and they were lazy as hell.

When the sheriff got to the rustlers' shack, the deputy who had remained behind told him that Fain and Garlock had headed south. Knowing the range of the rustlers' wagon, Sheriff Ed figured they almost had to be headed for the Flying W, one of the biggest ranches in southern Oklahoma. The road the rustlers had taken led to the northern boundary of the ranch about six miles away. They had hit this ranch before but didn't appear to have enough imagination to change their target.

Following section-line roads, the lawmen worked their way around so they could approach the Flying W from the south, on the same farm road the rustlers were traveling. Cattle could be seen grazing near the road. The sheriff and deputies pulled their car off the road and into a grove of trees. The car hidden, they spread out along the road in the ditches, which were filled with deep grass and weeds. Each of the deputies carried a Colt .44 pistol and Sheriff Ed had his Colt and a 12-gauge shotgun.

The plan called for them to wait for the rustlers, let them pull into the Flying W, and then follow them on foot to the herd. When the rustlers got set to kill a cow, they would put them under arrest.

"You boys be careful. We know one of 'ems got a rifle and the other's bound to be packin'," Sheriff Ed told his deputies.

The lawmen hadn't been hunkered down in the ditches for much more than an hour when the rustlers' wagon came down the road. They heard it and smelled the mules before they could see it.

The wagon passed them going south. Sheriff Ed let the wagon get about fifty yards ahead before he signaled his deputies to follow on foot. It was dark enough now that they could risk walking down the road, and the moon provided enough light that from time to time they could see the wagon's vague shape rolling slowly ahead.

After about a mile, the wagon stopped, and Sheriff Ed and his men would have likely walked up on the rustlers had not one of the deputies realized what was happening and saved them all by grabbing the sheriff's shoulder. The sheriff and his men slipped back into the bar ditch and regrouped, as they watched Fain use some wire cutters on the barbed-wire fence that separated the rustlers from the pasture and the grazing cattle. Garlock then led the mules off the road and into the pasture through the gap in the fence. Once inside, he walked right up to a steer and lit a kerosene lantern. The burst of light from it blinded the animal, leaving the steer transfixed as Fain shot it in the head with the .22.

They had him!

Sheriff Ed motioned the deputies forward, and guns drawn, they burst out of the dark.

"Drop your gun! You're under arrest!" Sheriff Ed shouted, covering Fain with his shotgun.

Instead, Fain whirled and fired at the sheriff. The shot went wild and Sheriff Ed let fly with a blast of 12-gauge shot that almost tore Fain's left leg in half.

Garlock threw his hands in the air and shouted, "Don't shoot!" As one of the deputies handcuffed Garlock, Sheriff Ed covered the rustler with his shotgun. Fain remained on the ground, bleeding profusely and in obvious pain. "Go get the car. We've got to get this guy to the hospital, even if he's not worth saving," the sheriff said.

* * * * *

A county commission meeting was in progress. All three commissioners were present, along with Sheriff Ed and the county attorney. The three commissioners sat together on one side of a conference table. The chairman, Paul Jones, sat in the middle and presided over the meeting. The county clerk was present to take notes. Since Sheriff Ed shot the rustler, Schroeder had been even more defensive and paranoid. He now refused to talk directly to the sheriff and had taken to complaining constantly about Sheriff Ed to the judge and the court clerk.

Right now, however, all Sheriff Ed wanted was two new cars for his department. He was standing before the commissioners to make that very request. "We've got to have two new cars," he told the commissioners. "That old buggy I'm driving barely runs, and the county is too big to cover with one car. Look at that rustler arrest, I had to borrow a second car from one of you guys. I found a good deal over in Ardmore. We can get two used Model Ts for $250 each. That's my request—two cars, five hundred bucks. I know that's a fair sum of money but I can't be out chasing some bank robber and have my car quit on me."

"Do I hear a motion to grant the sheriff's request?" Chairman Jones said.

"I object!" Schroeder said, jumping to his feet. "The sheriff doesn't do his job now. He certainly doesn't need a new car to do nothing. This is a waste of county funds."

"Sit down, Franz. We didn't ask for your opinion," Chairman Jones said.

Schroeder sputtered: "But I have to represent the people of this county. It is my legal duty to point out that the sheriff lets bootleggers, cockfighters, gamblers, and prostitutes run wild in this community. That shouldn't be rewarded with new cars."

Chairman Jones exhaled slowly and said, "Mr. Schroeder, the chair does not recognize you, and I'm tired of your interruptions."

"One more thing—!"

Before Schroeder could get another word out, Chairman Jones banged his gavel and said, "Sit down and shut up or I'll have Sheriff Ed put you out of the meeting. I'm sure he'd enjoy that."

"I see what's happening here!" Schroeder sputtered. "I'm tired of getting railroaded!"

With that, he stormed out of the meeting.

"Sorry about that, Ed," the chairman said.

"He's a tiresome little jerk but nothing more than a pest. I'd still like to have those cars though," Sheriff Ed replied.

"Do I hear a motion to approve the sheriff's request?" Chairman Jones asked. The motion passed unanimously.

"Thank you, Commissioners," Sheriff Ed said, as he gathered up his papers to leave. Then in the corner of his eye, a sudden motion. Schroeder was back, and this time he carried a revolver.

Without moving, Sheriff Ed said, "Drop the gun."

Schroeder did not comply.

"I said, drop the gun, Schroeder."

Instead, Schroeder lifted the gun and pointed it at the sheriff.

Three blasts exploded from Sheriff Ed's gun. One of the shots ricocheted off Schroeder's metal vest; one hit him in the groin; and the third, logged in the lawyer's leg. Schroeder staggered and fell.

"Call the doctor," Sheriff Ed told the county clerk. Then, he walked over to the chairman, handed over his gun, and said, "I'm turnin' myself in until this is all straightened out."

"That's not necessary, Ed," Chairman Jones said.

"Yes, it is," the sheriff said, as he leaned over to check on Schroeder. The attorney was bleeding a lot and groaning weakly, but he had a pulse.

"I can't believe he'd bring a gun in here," Chairman Jones said.

"I can't believe he intended to use it. Hell, I didn't want to shoot the son of a bitch but you saw it. He wouldn't drop the gun. He was set on using it," Ed said.

"Will he make it?" the chairman asked.

"I think so," Sheriff Ed replied.

But, in the end, he didn't.

* * * * *

Sheriff Ed walked into the house and threw his cowboy hat on the table.

"I think I'll have a drink of that illegal whiskey," he said.

"What's your excuse now that the county attorney's gone?" Maggie asked.

"Didn't think I needed one. Come wet your whistle."

"Don't mind if I do," his wife said. "I'm just glad the whole mess is over with."

"Well, there was no doubt it was self-defense. I had at least four witnesses. For all we know, he might have shot them too. Think he was crazy enough."

"I hate to say I told you so, but I told you so."

The sheriff raised his glass. "That's at least once you knew what you were talking about."

THE HOLDUP

. . . .

Nelda had to get out of this shithole job in this shithole town. Working in Eddie's liquor store for eight dollars an hour didn't cut it anymore. It hadn't always been this way. During the oil boom, waitressing in a local bar could pay off with plenty of big tips for a looker like Nelda.

Of course, that had also led to some poor decisions. Leroy came to mind. It was that smile of his that had gotten her. Whatever else he was, which wasn't much, Leroy had a killer smile. About her age, he was not quite handsome but damn that smile. He had a good job too, driving a truck for a drilling company out of Tulsa, and a fair line of bullshit.

They might have had a future but the bar closed when the oil business went in the shitter and drilling all but stopped. No need for drivers after that. Then Leroy upped and disappeared, *Boom and bust—you'd have thought it was the first time it had ever happened.*
leaving Nelda with a car payment she couldn't afford and a nine-month-old son. Boom and bust—you'd have thought it was the first time it had ever happened. Nelda marveled how no one ever seemed to see it coming. Western Oklahoma got gut-punched once again, and things only got worse thanks to a long drought that had crippled the wheat farmers. All those pickup trucks that still smelled of new

were repossessed by the banks and everybody who could leave town, did. This was no Great Depression or Dust Bowl but some days Nelda couldn't help wondering if this was how those times had felt.

Nelda hung on because she didn't have a choice. Her mom helped look after little Leroy, and she'd been able to find work, even if the job wasn't worth a damn. Boom or bust, people still drank, only now mostly beer and cheap whiskey. It helped that her boss Eddie had the only liquor store in town.

Eddie also rented out some trailer homes he owned. Nelda lived in one of them and so a big chunk of her paycheck went right back to the boss. The cheap motherfucker found ways to squeeze the money out of everything he touched. She didn't waste time complaining about it; she knew in times like this that she was one of the lucky ones. She still had a job and she knew she'd figure a way to get out of town, somehow. She wasn't dumb and at twenty-two, she still had the kind of body that made men look twice. If she didn't go out of her mind while she figured a way out, she'd be fine or, at least, that's what she kept telling herself.

* * * * *

Nelda was often the only one in the liquor store. Dressed in a T-shirt and jeans, she passed the time dusting the bottles and vacuuming or surfing the Internet. She expected to see Eddie pull in soon. He sometimes came in midafternoon but usually not until six or so, when he took over from her for the evening. Sometimes he showed up unannounced. Nelda was sure that was just to check the cash register to see if anything had gone missing, and, yep, here he came now.

Eddie was about sixty but looked older. Mostly bald, he was tall and thin, stooped-shouldered, with suspicious eyes. He always wore western shirts and cheap Walmart slacks, with a ring of keys that hung off his belt. He was fiddling with those keys when he walked in, and Nelda noticed he didn't look her in the eye as he came around behind the counter and opened the cash register.

"How's business?" he asked.

"Same as always. Lou bought a six-pack and Charley, a five-dollar bottle of wine. A couple of Mexicans bought two cases of beer and a bottle of Jim Beam. Maybe they'd robbed a bank."

Eddie didn't laugh but complained in a familiar whine: "Can't make any money on this place when it's open and can't make any money when it's closed."

"Yeah, yeah, yeah," Nelda replied.

"It's the damn government and the big oil companies. They control the price of oil. They don't give a damn about a small business man."

"The price will come back. It always does. Then you'll be rolling in dough again. You still got the first nickel you ever made anyway."

Eddie set off down an aisle pretending to look over the displays, but Nelda knew he was actually checking to see if any stock was missing. What an asshole, she thought, not for the first time.

Eddie returned to the counter, and as he opened the register, he looked at Nelda and said, "I've got to let you go."

"What the hell, Eddie, I work for nothin'. Where you

going to get anybody else for the slave wages you pay?"

"My cousin's boy needs a job. He'll work for minimum wage."

"You'd let me go for seventy-five cents an hour. You are a cheap bastard."

The sound of a junker car pulling in outside interrupted them, and they both turned and watched a young guy in a trucker cap and dark glasses make a beeline to the store. He strode straight up to the counter, and before Nelda or Eddie could say a word, pulled a revolver from behind his back and pointed it right at Eddie.

"Give me your damn money," the guy said.

Nelda took a step back as Eddie fumbled in the money drawer, saying, "Okay, okay, there's not much here!"

The robber twitched as if high on something. Eddie pulled some cash from the register. It looked to be less than a hundred bucks.

"Empty your pockets," the robber ordered Eddie.

The robber scooped up the register cash as Eddie pulled his wallet out and threw it on the counter. The wallet bulged with what Nelda could tell were big bills.

"I'll take your watch too," the robber said, with his gun still leveled at Eddie and one eye on Nelda.

As Eddie unbuckled his watch, Nelda said, "Hey, kid maybe this is what you came in for . . ." and yanked up her shirt, showing off her nice-looking boobs.

The robber's head swiveled to look at Nelda.

Eddie pulled a sawed-off .410 shotgun out from under the counter and let fly, blowing a hole in the robber's chest and knocking him over backwards to the ground.

The robber flopped for a moment where he landed and then stopped. Nelda walked around the counter, leaned down, and felt his neck for a pulse.

"Call the cops. I think he's dead."

Eddie pulled out his cell phone.

"You think your cousin's boy can do that for you," Nelda said.

JUSTICE, OKLAHOMA STYLE

· · · · · · · · · · · ·

Dave Thorn cooked meth. It was the family business but one not without risk. His daddy had blown himself up along with his trailer and a good hunting dog cooking, and Dave had done three years in Big Mac, himself. It was the cost of doing business, a very profitable business at that. Dave had always found it easier to accept those risks than the cut he had to pay the local sheriff. That stuck in Dave's craw every time he handed the money over to the sorry son-of-a-bitch, but it was better than jail and meant no one else could do business in Adair County. Dave tried to think of it as a franchise payment. *This country had been outlaw friendly as far back as Belle Starr and Jesse James.*

A big man with hard eyes and bad prison tattoos, Dave drove a new model Ford F-150 truck and owned forty acres of mostly worthless land on the side of one of Oklahoma's Cookson Hills—both thanks to meth. This country had been outlaw friendly as far back as Belle Starr and Jesse James. All these years later, the folks still had no use for the law, which served Dave just fine as he sat in his truck in the gravel parking lot behind Leon's Bar & BBQ, about a mile outside of Stilwell.

Dressed in a flannel work shirt, jeans, and cowboy boots, Dave watched the last drunk stagger out of the bar and weave away in a beat-up old truck. His watch read 2:00 a.m. A few minutes later, Leon's neon sign went dark, and then Ted, the bartender, came out and locked the door. Dave got out of his truck with a .38 revolver stuck in his belt behind his back, and headed toward Ted.

A tall, lanky kid with long blond hair wearing a Toby Keith T-shirt, Ted was tougher than he looked, known to have almost beaten a rowdy drunk to death with a baseball bat during his tenure at Leon's. He was one of Dave's best dealers too.

"You and me got to talk," Dave said.

Ted stopped but didn't respond.

"I heard you was buying from someone else."

"I'd say that was none of your damn business," Ted said.

Dave stepped toward Ted. A knife flashed in the kid's hand, slashing up and out at Dave's stomach. Quick for a big man, Dave sidestepped the knife and kicked hard at Ted's knee. Ted pitched forward and hit the ground. Dave kicked Ted hard in the head, and before Ted could even raise the knife, Dave stomped on Ted's hand with the heel of his cowboy boot. Dave could feel the bones in Ted's hand shatter as Ted let out a piercing scream. Dave kicked Ted again in the side, pulled his gun, and pointed it at Ted.

"You ever come at me again I'll blow your fuckin' head off. By the way, you're out of business shithead."

Dave walked back to his truck without a backward glance, but as he drove away, he saw Ted still on the ground, trying, with no success, to push himself up with his good hand.

* * * * *

Sheriff Dewey sat in his patrol car in the shade of an old Oak tree. He was parked on the shoulder of a little used dirt road that ran through hills too rocky to farm. A middle-aged man who looked older than he was, he had worn a badge for fifteen years, first as a small-town policeman, then as a deputy sheriff. Never much of a cop, he was good at politics, and so when the long-time sheriff died, he talked the county commissioners into giving him the job. There hadn't been a day since he took office that Dewey hadn't stolen or thought about stealing. He ripped off the jail's food allowance for the prisoners, padded his expense account, and took a cut on bail bonds. However, he learned fast that the real money was in drugs. Somebody was going to sell drugs and wiping them out was unrealistic, so he figured that he might as well be in the game. Meth was the redneck drug of choice in the hills and the sheriff knew that Dave cooked it, so it wasn't long before he cut himself in on the take.

The sheriff watched Dave's pickup roll down the road towards him and stop alongside his cruiser. Dave climbed out with a grocery bag and ambled over. "How's business?" the sheriff asked.

"Mostly good. Had a little trouble with that bartender over at Leon's, but I handled it," Dave replied.

"I heard the kid got mugged but couldn't identify who did it."

"Something like that," Dave said.

"So, let's settle up."

Dave frowned. "Your cut is too damn big. I do all the work and take all the chances, and you get 20 percent. That's too much."

"Whoa there, Pardner. This isn't a negotiation. Last I recall, you are a felon on parole. You're darn lucky I let you operate at all."

"I know the drill, but I also know that you're a greedy fucker, and if I go down, you go down too," said Dave.

"I'll pretend I didn't hear that," the sheriff said. "But tell you what, I'm a businessman so how about this: You bring in 20 percent more cash, and we'll talk about it. Now let's not sit around here any longer. Give me the take."

Dave hesitated then handed the sack through the window.

The sheriff grabbed the sack and put it on the passenger seat of his cruiser. As he rolled up his window and started the car, the sheriff gave Dave a little nod, "See you in Sunday School."

Dave shot him the finger and watched as the sheriff drove away.

* * * * *

Mayor Patton had taken a seat in the office of the sheriff across the desk from the man himself. The owner of three Sonic franchises, the mayor was a portly, pink-faced man, and way too smiley. Knowing that the mayor would cut your nuts off for a nickel, Sheriff Dewey hated the smiling but realized it was even more annoying when the mayor came with an agenda.

"Now listen, Sheriff, these drugs are a crisis. We've had what? Three overdoses already this year? You got to do something!"

Sheriff Dewey tried not to squirm in his seat. "We've made a few busts, Mayor, but it's tough to knock 'em out. It's a problem all over this country not just here in the Hills."

"It's here I'm worried about. What are *you* doing about it?"

"We're on the lookout all the time, but you don't understand what we're up against. These Mexican cartels are bigger than General Motors. They just keep pumpin' drugs into this country. What we need is for Trump to build his wall."

"I hear meth is home cookin'. You can't hang that on Mexicans."

"You can *hear* anything, but I think I'd know if it was comin' from around here."

"I don't care where it comes from—you'd better stop it! I'm catching heat over it, and so you're gonna be too."

"Well, Mayor, we'll heat up things the best we can."

The mayor smiled: "I know you'll try, Sheriff."

"Yes sir, Mr. Mayor."

* * * * *

Sheriff Dewey drove down the dirt road to the usual meeting place. Dave's truck was already there and Dave was sitting in the driver's seat. He appeared to be taking a nap. The sheriff pulled in facing the truck, nose to nose, and honked the horn.

Dave didn't move.

The sheriff shut off the car, got out, and walked over to Dave's window.

He looked in and gagged. Dave's throat had been slit from ear to ear, and he was covered in blood.

He also looked to be stone cold dead.

The sheriff walked back to his car, got in, and reached for the radio, then changed his mind, backed up, turned, and drove away.

GAMBLER'S LUCK

· · · · · · · · · · · ·

In the time of the nicks, Sputniks, and beatniks, the highway from Los Angeles to Las Vegas unfurled flat and fast but only two lanes wide. Bordered by vast expanses of rock, sand, scraggly mesquite, and cacti, with no speed limit, the road was designed to get any and all would-be gamblers with fat wallets into town and any and all losers with empty ones out as fast as possible. On any given Friday evening, high- and low-rollers crowded the highway, speeding toward whatever luck had in store for them, and this Friday in the spring of 1958 was no exception.

We were your average irresponsible, college students highballing it down from northern California, and then across the desert to gamble and raise all the hell we could fit into one weekend. Driving Bargie's Oldsmobile, we traded turns behind the wheel down U.S. Route 101, and then into Nevada and the ever increasing traffic. The Olds was one of those circa-1950 tanks, a monument to Detroit steel and the era when cars were big, powerful, and heavy and no one gave a damn about the price of gas or the miles per gallon. The Olds was a good running car that stuck to the road even at eighty-five miles per hour and operated best in a straight line, and so we were covering ground fast.

The Olds was one of those circa-1950 tanks, a monument to Detroit steel and the era when cars were big, powerful, and heavy and no one gave a damn about the price of gas . . .

Eventually, having run out of bad jokes and grown tired of the country and western station on the radio, we decided it was Sleeping

83

Beauty's time to drive. Tom had been sleeping off a hangover in the back seat for hours, waking only to beg for an Alka-Seltzer or pop to settle his stomach and raging thirst. It was a fluke Tom was there at all. He hadn't shown up that morning for departure, and we had debated whether to leave without him. We ended up opting, instead, for a run by his dump of an apartment. Even then, it took a good amount of yelling and door-pounding to wake him. He was still drunk from the night before and reeked of cheap booze but managed to stagger to the car, where he threw himself into the back seat and passed out with a few unintelligible gurgling sounds, so much for lively travel conversation. Our need for a driver trumped his need to recover, so we shook Tom awake and set about questioning him to see if he was able to drive. He passed our minimal sobriety test and off we headed back into traffic with Tom at the wheel.

Tom had no more taken over driving duties than he became frustrated by a slower car ahead of us and swung the Olds wide into the left lane to try and pass it, bringing us face to face with an eighteen-wheeler, thundering down the lane. Tom had time to swing back into the right lane or maybe even complete his pass but he chose neither. Instead, going seventy-five miles per hour, he chose to freeze side by side with the car we were in the middle of passing.

The truck driver laid on his horn but it was way too late to stop. We were hung out in the Nevada twilight, bound for glory. For some reason, I remained surprisingly calm, with an almost Zen-like acceptance of the situation. Bargie yelled something I don't recall, and at the last minute, Tom swerved further left, tearing into the desert spraying sand and gravel and leaving mutilated cacti in our wake. We ended up all three of us—the semi, the slow car, and the Olds—side by side, with the trucker still on his horn and the Olds fishtailing across the desert.

The Olds finally came to rest right side up, with a stunned Tom still behind the wheel of Bargie's car, but not for long. Bargie, still sitting shotgun, exploded. Screaming "you dumb son of a bitch," he dragged Tom out of the car and threw him down on the rocky desert floor. When Bargie's anger finally cooled a bit, I took over behind the wheel, and we got back on the highway, still headed to Vegas and still furious with Tom, whom we proceeded to verbally abuse all the way to Vegas.

We reached our destination alive and in one piece, in spite of Tom's efforts to the contrary. Securing lodging was next on the agenda. Our choice was the El Playtel, located behind the Desert Spa, which was behind the Desert Inn. I think the El Playtel even predated Bugsy Siegel. The place had a neon sign that didn't work and a gravel parking lot but the price was right—six dollars a night and they didn't complain that three of us would occupy a double room. Availability was no problem as the Rat Pack chose other accommodations.

Tom had started the drive rough but had arrived fresh as a daisy, having slept off his hangover and been rendered sober by our near-death experience on the highway. Bargie and I were, on the other hand, completely drained. With the resiliency of youth, however, we were soon hard at work shooting craps and playing blackjack, with indifferent success. We doggedly followed our plan to drink and gamble all night and then, after a few precious hours sleep, to catch The Tournament of Champions being played at the Desert Inn golf course.

This being Vegas, there was plenty of betting action available on the golf tournament. The big betting was taking place on the head-to-head matchups between the players, with the biggest money on the pairing of Arnold Palmer and Ken Venturi. Being from NorCal, we backed Ken. On Friday, the two men tied so they were paired again on Saturday. This was great for the bookies as almost everybody doubled down on their bets. Venturi won the match but not the tourney, which went to a great short-game artist and putter named Jerry Barber. Barber was known for his skills, but another tourney favorite was the Terrible Tempered Tommy Bolt, who was infamous for throwing golfing tantrums at the slightest provocation, but this time Tommy kept his cool—despite a lime green golf shoes and slacks ensemble that surely drew some commentary of its own; Tommy's attire was outdone only by the sartorial splendor of Doug Sanders dressed head to toe in bright orange.

By Saturday night, we were back at the gambling tables, and sometime in Sunday's early morning hours, I hit a hot streak at the roulette table betting on red. In 1954, the casinos still used silver dollars as chips, and I had more than four hundred of them stuffed in the pockets of my pants and sports coat, a jingling, jangling, walking silver piggy bank, rich for a day. Somehow I managed to get out of town with most of my winnings and a few stories to tell the boys back at school; we headed north with, of course, Bargie and me taking turns doing the driving.

We didn't see Tom much after that excursion until the day he invited us both over to witness the trial firing of an antitank gun he had ordered by mail from an advertisement in the back of *Popular Science* magazine. This was long before the present angst over firearms, federal gun laws, or the problems with terrorism, and plenty of firepower was available on the open market. The gun itself was a relic of World War II, a small artillery weapon supposedly powerful enough to stop a tank. I don't remember the caliber but the thing set up on a tripod and fired a good-sized shell.

Tom set the gun up in the middle of campus and aimed it at a dry lake bed about a half mile away. The only problem with his target was that a dormitory for girls sat right in the line of fire, about a hundred yards away from us. Tom's shot needed to clear the dorm to hit the target. After a last review of the instructions, Tom fired off a live round. Remarkably, his calculations proved correct! The shell missed the dorm and hit the lake dead center, creating a great explosion of mud and debris. This of course was cause for a great drunken celebration. Tom proved not so lucky later, when the school officials took umbrage to his warlike tendencies and, invited him to leave school permanently, hardly justified one could argue, in view of his accurate marksmanship.

Not long after that, high on cheap wine and a beautiful Mexican girl that danced at Sinaloa, I wandered into a North Beach alley in San Francisco only to be confronted by Jack Kerouac and Jomo Kenyatta. Kenyatta had a bloody machete on his hip and the severed head of a white Kenyan farmer tied to his belt. He glared in my direction, and I shot him the finger. He just kept on walking, trying to listen to Kerouac's ramblings, as we all kept moving along our different paths to eternity. That was when I understood why I was so calm when facing death on the highway in Nevada. I was both invisible and invincible, an imaginary condition, that was soon proven false.

My attitude didn't help me keep my four hundred dollars either. I bet all I had left on Silky Sullivan in the tenth at Bay Meadows, one of the few times the greatest come from behind horse of all time, couldn't, and regardless of what other qualities I might or might not possess, permanent good luck wasn't one of them.

ROSE

When I first met her, I didn't know it would end like it did but then you never do. She was sitting by the red rock trail crying—not because her mother had died but because she had just had a second flat and did not have another spare. I stopped and asked if she needed help. She looked up at me with a mud-splattered face and said, "Fuck off." As I pedaled away, she hoisted her bike over her shoulder and started down the trail, muttering to herself.

I saw her next at the trailhead and asked if she wanted to have a beer. She asked if I was "out of my mind," but after a second look she started to laugh, almost a cackle, and said, "If you're buyin' I'm drinkin'." We went to a restaurant in Moab. The fucking Mormons don't allow bars, but they'll sell you whiskey out of state-owned package stores, and restaurants can serve drinks. She said her name was Rose because she was one *thorny bitch*, but I never knew for sure if that was her name.

She asked me what I liked to do beside bike, and I said, "Read."

She said, "I like to read too."

I asked her, "What kind of books do you read?"

She said, "*The Kama Sutra*."

We ended up in my rented trailer house and two months later she moved in.

She was a small, wiry woman, not so much pretty as athletic-looking, with intense dark eyes. To be frank, most of the time she looked a little crazy and she was. You might have guessed that she would have tattoos but she didn't. When I asked why, she looked at me as if I were crazy.

"I wouldn't let some bastard stick a dirty needle full of ink in me," she said.

She liked to smoke weed and when she did she liked to dance. That's the way I best remember her, a little bit stoned, dancing in front of the trailer house, on a starry high desert night, with Lady Gaga playing on the boom box and me sitting in my worn out lawn chair drinking beer and taking it all in. Well, either that or on her bike, somewhere between fearless and out of control, taking the fastest way down, in the air more than on the ground, flying, in her dirt-covered bike shorts and well-worn jersey. Biking was what she lived for in this world. The rest of her life was just the time spent between rides, nothing else really mattered, including me.

What happened between us was so quick and unexpected, I still don't really believe it ever happened—to have what you want one day and then have it gone the next, to stare at the red rock vistas that haven't changed but suddenly leave a hollow lump in your stomach because that's where she used to be and isn't anymore.

Now here, and then gone.

A ghost that won't leave me alone.

FATHER'S DAY

· · · · · · · · · · · ·

I remember the last words my father said to me: "You come in here, you son of a bitch, and I'll blow your ass off." Spoken while holding his 12-gauge, pump shotgun, sitting in his favorite, badly worn, red velvet armchair, surrounded by stacks of old newspapers, plates of half-eaten food, and empty beer cans. The room was half dark, with the shades drawn. The place had that musty smell that comes with old houses and old people.

He had already threatened Marilyn, the woman who occasionally looked in on him, and the police that now waited outside the house trying to avoid a confrontation with a deluded old man. I had persuaded them to let me try to talk to him, even though Marilyn warned me that "he's been getting worse and worse." I understood what she meant. There had been plenty of signs of his deterioration: Forgetfulness, long periods of silence, and then sudden violent rages. Quiet and morose even in the best of times, he had graduated from cynical to bitter and then, to brooding. But this was new.

He had seemed under control until about a year ago, when he attacked the Baptist minister in the Walmart parking lot. The minister and several parishioners had been handing out flyers inviting people to a church event. Dad was there to pick up a few things. He'd insisted on going in the store though Marilyn had discouraged it, and then, when the preacher tried to hand Dad a flyer, all hell broke loose: "Get away from me, you sanctimonious son of a bitch!" were his exact words.

"No need for that kind of language sir," the preacher replied.

"Don't lecture me, you pompous piece of shit," Dad said.

Marilyn told me he glared at the preacher then, and when the man started to speak again, Dad decked him and started stomping on the fella. It had taken two of the parishioners and a security guard to pull Dad off the minister and hold him until the cops arrived.

When I arrived, the one thing I knew for sure was that whatever had had happened, it had nothing to do with the preacher's particular church affiliation. One thing you could say about my dad, he treated all religions the same, with equal disgust. To him, the Pope, ISIS, and the Dalai Lama—all the same. I remember watching a war movie on TV with him when I was a boy. One of the characters said, "There are no atheists in foxholes," and Dad blurted out, Bullshit!" Mom shushed him, but there was no doubt how he felt.

After the Walmart attack, I had to bail Dad out of jail and get him a lawyer. Dad being a veteran, an insincere apology, and the preacher's good-heartedness kept the judge from sending the old man to jail. From that point on, things had only gotten worse. Each day seemed to bring a marking in a life long ago over but refusing to end. There was no question about institutionalizing him. He wasn't about to go, and no one wanted to try to make him leave the small, white frame house where he had lived for more than forty years.

In spite of all his problems both health and otherwise, I had always been able to reason with my dad, maybe because I was his favorite, ever since I bloodied Jimmy Clark's nose in the third grade. Sometimes even now, he would listen to me, even as the paranoia and dementia grew worse.

As I looked at him across the darkened room, he was still a formidable man. Although slumped forward and beginning to shrink, like old men do, Dad retained a powerful neck and shoulders that could swell with the anger he carried still against his enemies, most of them long dead. That air of strength reminded me of those times as a boy when I would see him chopping wood, maniacally bringing the ax down again and again as though the logs had personally wronged him. I don't know if the anger was always there or if it was part of his fear and loathing for the war he wouldn't talk about but could never forget. I do know the anger stayed with him as close as the jagged V-shaped scar on his back.

"Dad, it's me, Charles," I said from the door of the room.

His only reply was a grunt that may or may not have been "ass-hole," as the gun swung up, pointing in my general direction.

I had just enough time to dive away, before he fired off a wild blast that tore a huge hole in the living room wall. Then things went really crazy: Policemen rushing into the house. Someone roughly jerking me aside. Yelling, and the sound of running feet. My dead mom's precious ceramic clock crashing to the floor; pieces of it skidding everywhere. The screen door torn off the wall. The shotgun roaring out again. The smell of gunpowder and blood. My shoulder hurting from where I'd hit the floor. A taste of steel in my mouth. One policemen cursing and another saying, "the old bastard had to do it."

Someone tried to help me to my feet, but I didn't really want to get up. It was too late.

THE PIANO PLAYER

· · · · · · · · · · · ·

Once upon a time in the old West, there lived a piano player who was possessed of one remarkable talent: He could play and sing "Swing Low, Sweet Chariot" better than anyone else in the world. His rendition of the spiritual could make hardened cowboys cry openly and leave women weeping for days afterward. Although the piano player could play other tunes too, his unique and unmatchable ability to mesmerize an audience was confined to this one Christian hymn.

As time passed, his fame spread throughout the American West, and he was able to make a living performing the song, going from town to town, playing mainly in saloons and churches, which were about the only places where pianos could be found. No tickets were needed to hear him play. He was paid in tips and the best available whiskey and food, and by the standards of the times, lived very well.

One hot and dusty day, the piano player found himself in the south Texas town of Falfurrias, not too far from the Mexican border. He was playing in a saloon before a crowd of patrons who had come just to hear the piano player play "Swing Low, Sweet Chariot." Present in the saloon too that day was the noted killer and bandit Charlie the Dog, a nickname acquired because most days Charlie smelled like a dog and, in fact, always looked somewhat like an ugly pitbull bulldog. Rumor had it that Charlie had killed more than one hundred men, more than half with his barehands. He was never without a long-barreled, 44 caliber, hogleg pistol, he wore strapped to one leg or the bowie knife, that graced the other. Like all good serial killers, he had an I.Q. of about seventy. Charlie was big and brutal, stupid and thoroughly mean. On this particular occasion, he was also skunk drunk, which made him stick out from the rest of the convivial crowd. Indeed, even the piano player had noticed Charlie in the crowd, though he was confused by the hostile looks Charlie kept sending his way. Having drawn the stares of thousands of mean drunks in his years of performing on the road, the piano player did not pay too much attention to Charlie; instead, he continued to play a string of warm-up songs. Before he could finish warming up, however, Charlie stood and bellowed in a loud, drunken voice, "I understand you can play some song better than anyone in the world. Play that song now and you better play your best or I'll kill you."

With that, Charlie drew his huge hogleg gun.

"Play!" he commanded the piano player.

Needing no more encouragement, the piano player turned back to the piano and began to sing, "Swing low, sweet chariot . . ." As his fingers tickled the ivories, the piano player was not worried; after all, he was the best in the world and he had seen men tougher than Charlie sob like babies when they heard him sing his song. So, the piano player just carried on.

He played and he sang, and he sang and he played. As he did, he could feel his gift, as always, begin to transfix the crowd. A mystical quiet fell over the room as one and all were slowly transported by the sweetness of his song. The piano player could almost see the people in the crowd vowing to become better versions of themselves before the chariots came to take them home. Purer and more melodious than the trilling of any bird, true to the music and the words, the piano player carried the crowd out of the harshness of reality into a state of transcendental delight; a few in the crowd would later swear they had seen the outline of the pearly gates.

All, that is, but one.

All, but Charlie.

As the last notes of the song wafted out the window into the blue Texas sky, so clear and fine no other mortal could ever duplicate them—and before the piano player could catch his eye again, the bandit known as Charlie the Dog drew his huge gun and fired.

A collective gasp rose from the room. Charlie had shot the piano player right between the eyes, splattering blood and brains all over the piano and killing the piano player instantly.

To the frightened faces all around him, Charlie only shrugged and said, "Son of a bitch pissed me off."

He then moved to the bar and demanded more whiskey.

Since it was two days' ride to the nearest sheriff, and no one wanted to call out Charlie on what he had done, the bartender simply removed the body of the piano player from the saloon to be buried later, and business went on as usual. Charlie continued to drink and later that night broke the neck of another customer with one blow of his huge right hand.

Some years later, Charlie the Dog would become the sheriff of a town in New Mexico. He lived to be eighty-eight years old. He died not from a bullet or the knife or a blow but from choking on a chicken bone.

Believe it or not, there is a moral to this story: "You can't please everybody so you better please yourself."

WAR

· · · · · · · · · · · ·

Danny was in a hurry and it was rush hour on a Friday. That meant lots of traffic as people fled their offices for the weekend. He needed to get started as soon as possible if he was gonna catch the crowd. Knowing this, he had ridden his bicycle home as fast as he could from work, even leaving a few minutes early from the bookstore, which always pissed off the manager. He'd covered the three miles back to his apartment in less than ten minutes. From his apartment to the corner where he liked to stand was less than a mile and he would be there soon. The weather wasn't good, windy and spitting snow, but he had been out in worse. He sometimes lived in worse. His apartment was often cold. The landlord, a cheap bastard, always kept the heat as low as possible.

The apartment wasn't even much to look at either—only three small, but tall, rooms in an old building dating back to the 1940s, a little shabby but not bad for the rent. He'd furnished the rooms with garage-sale finds and an old television set bought at a flea market; he kept the place orderly, one of the good habits he had picked up in the army. There was no reason to have a nicer place, which he couldn't have afforded anyway; he had few visitors, and when he got together with the older woman who lived down the hall, it was always at her place. She liked to do it in her bed and then make tea afterwards; on weekends sometimes, they'd drink cheap wine and listen to her stereo.

Having missed lunch, he was hungry and grabbed a handful of pretzels as he changed into his old fatigues and put on a stocking cap, gloves, and a heavy parka. He grabbed his handwritten sign and made sure the cardboard placard was firmly nailed to its wooden handle. The sign read:

Get us out of Iraq.
Why are we there anyway?

The words on the sign had changed some over the weeks that he'd been displaying it, but the message remained the same.

He paused briefly in the doorway before leaving the apartment, trying to remember why he kept on doing what he did. If someone had asked him, he knew what his answer would be: It helped him sleep. On the evenings after he'd been out on the street sharing his message with the world, the explosions didn't go off in his dreams as much and he didn't see the mangled bodies as often. Even his leg didn't hurt as much on those nights. Now that he'd given up the pain pills, he needed something, and this was it.

Most of his friends told him that he was crazy or wasting his time, or both, but still he kept on protesting the war. At first, he had been able to convince others to help, but they'd gradually lost interest too. The heavyset girl with the bad complexion wouldn't be back. She hadn't shown up for three weeks and hadn't bothered to call. His friend Ike had gotten a better job and moved to another neighborhood, one too far, Ike said, to make the trip feasible. A few others who once had seemed interested, no longer came around.

As he headed out, Danny decided to walk instead of bike. It was easier to carry the sign walking than trying to control it on his bike with the wind blowing so hard. He hustled through his neighborhood, drawing what he had come to call "The Look" from the only person he passed on the street, an older woman in a stocking cap and scarf. He was used to The Look from neighbors, just as he was with The Finger from the drivers who drove by, and The Question from strangers that was always some play on: "If you don't like it here, why don't you get out of the country?" All three were better than the universal complacency about Iraq he faced daily. Most people were oblivious to the war. It was like the war was imaginary, not even fought by real people.

Why didn't they pay attention? He asked himself this all the time; it was part of what kept him up at night. People were getting killed and having their legs and brains blown up, and the war was costing billions of dollars, and yet, no one seemed to care.

Well, he cared.

Danny reached the busy intersection and assumed position on the median facing the homebound traffic flowing out of downtown toward the suburbs. The intersection was controlled by stoplights— so the traffic had to stop and the drivers could hardly miss his sign, even if they were on their cell phones or had the radio on. The temperature had dropped since he left the apartment, and the wind had picked up. Danny paced up and down the median trying to stay warm but still shivering in the cold wind.

He had been on the corner only a few minutes when he noticed a car, a new black Lexus, slow down and the driver take a long look in his direction as the car continued up the street. Danny did a double take when the Lexus made a U-turn, came back in the opposite direction, and turned into the parking lot across the street. He watched the driver get out of the sedan and start in his direction. The driver was a big, square-shouldered, middle-aged man with a thick neck, wearing an expensive-looking blue overcoat and leather gloves. He hustled through traffic and headed straight for Danny. He had the florid face of someone who drinks or has high blood pressure; Danny smiled as he noticed some snowflakes sticking to the man's hair. The driver didn't look happy but the snowflakes took the edge off. Or they did, until the man reached Danny and barked: "What's your name?"

"Danny Watson."

"Are you a vet, Son?"

"Yes, Sir." Danny said.

"When I came home from Nam, there were a bunch of pansy-ass cock-sucking, draft dodgers protesting the war. I hated all of them. I wanted to beat the shit out of every single one of them."

Danny wasn't sure where this was going or what to say in return, but before he could figure it out, the man said, "But, you know what, those pricks were right."

"Yes, they were," Danny said.

"Keep up the good work, Danny Watson," the driver said as he extended his hand.

Danny returned the man's powerful grip, and the driver turned and hurried back to his car through the drifting snow.

THE SUBSEQUENT ORAL CONTRACT

In the days before the curse of the billable hour, being chosen to be an associate in a law firm was considered a coup. Deemed lucky to have the opportunity to learn to practice law while getting paid, young lawyers made less than legal secretaries. On the other hand, they were thought of as professionals not the money-making cash machines they are today.

Given this, I was pleased to cast my lot with what was then considered to be a large established firm of nine lawyers, all of whom, save for one other neophyte, were partners. I think I got the job because I was a veteran and one of the partners went to high school with my mother. In any event, I was glad to have the position.

The partners were a diverse lot, and while they seemed to get along for the most part, it was hard to understand how they had gotten together in the first place. Later, I would come to think of law firms as amoebas, constantly separating and then rejoining in parts, usually over questions of money or clashes of egos. I also learned firms of any size can contain strange combinations of personalities. Few, however, more seemingly different than the senior partners in the outfit that I first joined.

One senior partner, Fisher, was the epitome of Ivy League conservatism. A graduate of Harvard and an ex-naval officer, he was punctual to a fault, and his habits were robotically routine. He arrived every day at the same time, ate lunch at the same time, and left at the same time. His practice consisted almost entirely of rendering oil-and-gas title opinions, a job he performed with meticulous accuracy, using an ancient hand-cranked adding machine that produced voluminous tapes filled with strings of endless decimal computations. An austere man, always well-dressed in gray or dark blue suits, his only known pleasure was attending hockey games, having been spotted in a box near rink side at every game ever played in Oklahoma City, always wearing a fedora. His everyday stature was military erect; his everyday lunch was taken at a private club at the same round table with several arch conservative business leaders. His lunch crowd included the president of the city's largest bank and the infamous (and powerful) publisher of the city's only daily newspaper. Fisher ate the same lunch everyday: roast beef, peas, and mashed potatoes. Although it was rumored that business deals were made at these lunches, the conversation more likely was spent on the graduated income tax, which these men had never accepted as constitutional.

The firm's other senior partner, Phil, made for a startling contrast. Hawk-nosed with dark intelligent eyes, he was that unique breed: an uncommon, common man. His law degree was earned in a one-year crash course from Cumberland University in Tennessee. Prone to wearing ugly sports coats, he was self-made in every sense of the word. Prior to practicing law, he had worked as an auto and airplane mechanic. He was a veteran of the Army Air Corps, and loved flying his own plane, even though serious questions existed about his eyesight. An ex-assistant district attorney, he had a rough-and-tumble trial practice, with clients often hiring him as a result of his active involvement in Democratic politics.

I knew right away that I hadn't become a lawyer to sit in an office examining titles and gravitated to Phil, who always had plenty of clients and whose practice involved a wide variety of cases, including contested probate estates, an acrimonious and lucrative line of work. Estate cases were fraught with human interest, greed, and animosity. As many lawyers know, there is no hatred quite like that between family members. Introduce substantial assets that are not distributed as the beneficiaries' expected, and every petty slight, insult, or family feud will be resurrected, magnified, and used to bludgeon the other party.

Early on, Phil had me help him represent a client named Lucky. Lucky was the alleged illegitimate son of a rancher who lived in the Oklahoma Panhandle; this being before DNA, Lucky's parentage was hotly contested when the rancher died. Lucky's father had met his demise in a hotel in Perryton, Texas, where, after a weekend of drunken revelry, he had poured himself a tub of cold water, intended to induce sobriety. Unfortunately, when the rancher leapt into the tub, the shock was too great for his heart, which promptly stopped beating. A good fast way to go, but the rancher left behind an unexpected mess for his three legitimate sons and our client, the infant Lucky. Matters were further complicated because one of the sons was in the middle of a divorce.

As for the stakes, they were high. The family ranch not only maintained a large cattle herd but also many producing gas wells and a valuable pit of caliche, a raw material used in construction worldwide. The first hearing took place in Perryton, over the entitlement to a Texas bank account of the then princely sum of $200,000; twelve lawyers showed up representing conflicting interests. The battle over the estate raged on for the two and a half years I worked for the firm, and then into the future, culminating after ten years in a settlement for Lucky and a predictable dispute between lawyers over attorney fees, reminiscent of *Jarndyce v. Jarndyce* in Charles Dickens's *Bleak House*.

Which leads me to the story of what I consider my first real jury trial. Although not a probate case, it was typical of the diverse cases Phil attracted. I had already tried a case before a six-man jury in Justice of the Peace court, but that one never gave off any Perry Mason vibes, even though my client's auto supply company miraculously prevailed in a suit brought by an irate customer, despite the credit manager, without any apparent legal authority, having gone to the customer's residence, jacked up his car, and removed the two back tires. The customer had refused to pay because of a perceived defect in the tires and then unwisely taunted the credit manager over the phone. Oklahomans have always had a tendency to self-help and frontier justice.

I came away with a win in the case, but my first *real case* would be a full scale trial before a jury of twelve in the Oklahoma County Courthouse. The Honorable Judge Carl Traub would preside over the trial in the Court of Common Pleas, a great name for a court, that no longer exists, wiped out by subsequent court reform. I was, of course, looking forward to the trial save for one important thing, my client was the local Chrysler, Plymouth, and Dodge dealership owned by a huckster named Les. Some years previously, Phil had purchased a Chrysler from Les, and they had cut a deal. Phil could trade up for a new Chrysler each year without any additional cost and Les had carte blanche legal services from Phil's law firm.

Like any good car dealer, Les was a cheap chiseler, and abused the deal by seeking legal counsel on every problem, no matter how small, and suing over the least perceived wrong. Given this, Les was always assigned to the newest associate, and the associate preceding me had eagerly turned over all of Les's files to me on my first day at the firm. To make matters worse, Les was never satisfied with the legal service rendered and complained about the quality of any associate's work. Working for Les was sort of the KP of law practice, something you only did because you wanted to keep the job.

In this case, my assignment for Les was to represent him in a dispute with a laundry business. The owner of the laundry, Al, had leased two vans from Les's dealership for two years. The terms of the lease required that upon the return of the vehicles, they were to be sold and an additional amount would be due to the dealership, based on a formula for depreciation and the sales price received for the vans. According to Al, at the end of the original term, he had made a deal with Les's sales manager to extend the lease one year and waive any deficiency that might occur due to the sales price brought by the vehicles. This deal unfortunately was verbal, and the sales manager had inconveniently decided to die before the extended term had expired. Les sold the vehicles, and in doing so, established a debt of some four thousand dollars. Les denied the existence of any such deal outside the terms of the written lease. When Al refused to pay, Les sued. With Les, compromise or retreat was never on the table since he had, in effect, a free lawyer.

In preparing for trial, I had hoped to rely on the Dead Man's Rule, which excludes testimony about conversations with a deceased person. However, I quickly learned that an exception to this rule existed when the conversations were with the agent or employee of a corporation, and under this exception, Al was free to testify about his dealings with the dead sales manager.

My next thought was the Parole Evidence Rule, which prohibits the altering of a written contract by oral agreements, but unfortunately, the rule does not apply to a subsequent oral contract but only to prior or contemporaneous oral agreements. Al's counsel, the venerable Stubbs, was well aware of this exception. Stubbs was a countrified, somewhat bewildered-looking man, who was smarter than he looked. While Les was, of course, relying on the written lease, Stubbs, from the start of the trial, pounded on his client's agreement with the dead sales manager as a "subsequent oral contract." We had no way of denying Al's assertion in this regard, other than to point out that the subsequent agreement had never been reduced to writing, and that no record of it other than Al's testimony existed.

When all the testimony had been received, the judge instructed the jury and closing arguments were made. Once again, Stubbs repeatedly referenced the *subsequent oral contract*.

After an hour or so of deliberation, a seemingly lengthy amount of time for such a relatively uncomplicated case, the jury rang for the bailiff, who was given a note to take to the judge. Judge Traub, a patient and quiet man, then called the lawyers to his office for a conference. Without disclosing his feelings, the judge passed me the handwritten note from the jury and inquired, "Counselor, how do you suggest I reply to this request?"

The note, which I am not likely to forget, stated:

Please send us a copy of the subsequent oral contract.

After some argument, the judge responded to the jury that, "You have heard all of the evidence necessary to decide this case. Please continue your deliberations." Another hour passed before the jury finally signaled that a verdict had been reached; the jurors were then led into the courtroom by the bailiff. The verdict was read aloud with the jury finding in favor of the defendant. The vote was eleven to one and the one was royally mad. Afterward, the dissenting juror approached me in the hall. "I told them and told them a contract is a contract," the obviously exasperated woman said, "and they didn't have no contract. If it wasn't written down, it wasn't no contract, your client should have won."

Naturally, I agreed.

Defeated and crestfallen, I returned to the office to face the unenviable task of informing Phil of my loss and to await the abuse that would inevitably be heaped on me by Les. As I entered the office, one of the younger partners stopped me to inquire about the outcome of the case, forcing me to reluctantly recite the sad story of the trial. I was taken aback when he burst out laughing upon hearing the verdict. To my further astonishment, once he stopped laughing, he led me around to office after office, proclaiming my legal prowess to everyone.

Seemed that rather than being a complete failure, I was the first lawyer in the firm who had ever gotten a single juror to vote for Les. Although a pyrrhic victory at best, the case did begin my education on why it is so difficult to predict the outcome of jury trials and the unexpected reasons why juries decide cases.

THE DOC AND ME

· · · · · · · · · · · ·

The Doc had gotten himself a new nemesis: the dreaded Urban Renewal Authority of the Department of Housing and Urban Development, or HUD. I learned this from Doc after he burst into my office, unannounced of course. To the Doc, a lawyer was like a six-gun, you kept it handy to draw quick when someone needed killing. In this case, that would be his archenemy, the bureaucratic forces of the United States government. Doc wasn't alone in his dislike of the heavy-handed tactics of the Urban Renewal Authority. The agency had hit town in the early Sixties and used the wrecking ball to tear down homes and buildings all over the near eastside of the city. Its bureaucrats had then moved on to condemn downtown properties, with, as of yet, still no signs of redevelopment in sight, leaving behind a swath of devastation and unhappy landowners. At least this time, Doc had found the right lawyer.

Doc wasn't alone in his dislike of the heavy-handed tactics of the Urban Renewal Authority.

When I became aware of the Urban Renewal Authority, my first reaction had been to scoff at what to me clearly appeared to be an unconstitutional federal program. Why, every law student quickly learns that the taking of private property for private uses is illegal in our country, not to mention immoral and bad for your digestion, and that's what Urban Renewal did. Of course, it was done under the guise of eliminating urban blight for the health, welfare, and benefit of all of the people. A tenuous theory, but one, I learned, after some hours of research in dusty law books, that had been upheld by none other than a number of federal judges across the country. That might have made it legal, but as far as I was concerned, it damn sure didn't make it right.

To take a man's property by condemnation against his will, and turn right around and sell it to another private individual for development, violated any sense of fundamental fairness and opened the door for corruption and influence peddling. My belief in this regard was further fueled by my original mentor in legal practice, who fought off the condemnation of his small downtown office building for almost twenty years. A World War II veteran, his contempt for the condemnation process was exacerbated by the fact that the master plan for our city was drawn up by I.M. Pei, whom he always referred to as "the Jap," having never quite forgiven the Japanese for the Great War. Given this background, when the Doc plopped down in front of me and unceremoniously interrupted whatever other business I was conducting, I was interested in his plight but wary too.

You may remember the Doc, a one-man investment company, who fit a medical practice around his free wheeling real estate and oil and gas investments. He was one of those people who counted every dollar, no every penny, even when it began to add up to millions. So tight was he that in his seventies the Doc had looked around his house one day and determined that it was simply too big for two people, those two people including his long-suffering wife. Having reached this conclusion, he went about having a wall constructed down the middle of their residence so that he could rent half of the house out as a duplex.

As far as his medical practice, the Doc was a general practitioner. To him, that meant he could do anything. Probably competent in giving routine medical advice, he was nonetheless fearless, or perhaps foolhardy, in undertaking complicated medical procedures, with little or no training. He once proudly performed a sex change operation before the procedure had been heard of in most of the U.S.

Fortunately, he did so in an era in which malpractice suits were rare and the medical profession was still revered by most people.

* * * * *

After clicking his false teeth a few times to get warmed up, the Doc began his latest quest.

"I've got a mortgage on this perfectly good house over on Eighth Street, near Walnut. The owner is a fine old Negro, named Ace, who shines shoes at my barbershop. He's never missed a payment. Now, this damned Urban Renewal bunch is condemning the house and won't pay enough to cover my mortgage. You've got to stop them!"

My next few minutes were spent convincing the Doc that this great federal bulldozer could not be stopped. Only then, was I able to explain that what we could do was contest the amount paid for the house. Somewhat mollified, he calmed down enough to plot a strategy to punish his adversary in the way that would gratify him the most: extracting money against their will.

First on the agenda was a trip to view what Doc kept referring to as the "perfectly good house" and meet its exalted owner, Ace. We pulled into a neighborhood that looked something like London a few years after the war. Most of the houses had already been torn down and the lots graded flat. Where once had been trees, sidewalks, lawns, and small residences, was now largely dust and bits of old foundations. Here and there a few holdouts, like Ace, formed small islands of a once somewhat rundown but still serviceable housing addition.

In spite of his oppression at the hands of the federal government, the Doc was in a particularly ebullient mood. He had just learned that Las Vegas was ceasing the use of silver dollars for gambling. The casinos were selling $1,000 silver coins for $1,100. Bearing in mind that these were real silver dollars, the Doc was headed to Vegas to buy $10,000 worth for $11,000. He tried to convince me to let him buy me a thousand too, but unlike the Doc, I didn't totally distrust the

U.S. economy and at that time a $1,000 dollars was a lot of money to invest. "Silver and gold are always worth something, even in a depression. I'm buying 'em and putting 'em in my safety deposit box," he said. "Just the silver in the coins is worth more than I'm paying." Unconvinced at the time, I often wondered later, while watching the price of silver climb, how much that $10,000 was now worth. I knew it multiplied in the Doc's favor many times over, not to mention the increase in the collector's value of some of the coins.

When we reached Ace's humble abode, I was pleasantly surprised to find it as described. Although in need of painting, the house was modest and well kept, and the yard was even mowed. Ace, himself, was a slight, gnarly-looking old man with gray hair and a stooped posture. He and the Doc had at least one thing in common: They were both hard of hearing. After a few shouted greetings back and forth, Ace invited us in.

The house's furniture and furnishings were clean but threadbare. Ace sat in what appeared to be his favorite easy chair, and I pulled a table chair in front of him and began to talk in a loud voice about his legal rights.

After some attempts at conversation, it became apparent that Ace was hopelessly confused about everything dealing with Urban Renewal. He did not understand how they could be "takin' his house," especially when he sure as hell didn't want to sell or move it. He was in denial despite the fact that Urban Renewal had already torn down his local grocery store and leveled most of the homes of his neighbors flatter than a tornado could. Unfortunately, without a car, Ace conceded that he couldn't hang on much longer. He seemed to be, as described: a reliable, likable old man who was simply being victimized by his own government to profit some well-connected developers in the name of all mighty progress.

Since the offer to purchase was less than the mortgage, I had to explain that I couldn't represent both the Doc and him, and that he needed a lawyer. Ace said he had already contacted a lawyer, a man named Doyle who had been recommended to him by his cousin. Known mainly as a criminal defense lawyer, Doyle had the gift of gab and was never troubled much by the law. With long, wavy hair and a sunny personality, he made a good mouthpiece for his clients in some circumstances, but Doyle knew absolutely nothing about condemnation law, which didn't seem to bother him a bit but did make him glad to have another lawyer on his side who could do the heavy lifting. Doyle and I got along well as the case proceeded toward trial, but we did have one problem: We needed an expert witness to testify as to the value of Ace's house. Almost all of the qualified appraisers in the city had worked, did work, or wanted to work for Urban Renewal. By offering a large volume of lucrative business the federal government had pretty much captured the appraisal community, giving local appraisers either a conflict of interest or a deep reluctance to oppose the government and possibly eliminate the hope of future appraisal work.

I told the Doc about the problem.

"No problem. Talk to Harvey; he'll know somebody," Doc said.

Harvey was the Doc's ace-in-the-hole, a longtime employee of the county assessor's office, who moonlighted by taking care of Doc's real estate, a good part-time job for a low-paid bureaucrat. Through no coincidence, Doc's properties were all assessed at the low end of any reasonable value for the computation of property taxes. Harvey was only too glad to help the Doc and as predicted had a good idea to contribute to the cause.

"I'll talk to Leon and see if he'll help," Harvey said.

Come to find out, Leon was not an appraiser; however, he was a licensed realtor and had handled a number of sales and negotiations with Urban Renewal. A stout black man who wore a three-piece suit and a bowler hat, he understood the game being played, and wanted to help Ace get what money could be got from his property. Leon quickly put a value on the house, three times that of the government's experts.

But would Leon be able to testify? The Urban Renewal lawyers objected on the grounds that he was unqualified. Fortunately, the judge bought my argument that any lack of education or actual training was offset by his personal experience dealing in local real estate. It didn't hurt that the judge and his family-owned property in the downtown area, and he didn't think much of Urban Renewal either. It also turned out that this was the first time in Oklahoma that an Urban Renewal condemnation case had actually gone to trial, and the judge had quickly become intrigued with the case and wanted to find out how a jury would treat Urban Renewal.

As the trial approached, Doyle and I worked out our strategy. We both voire dired the jury and made opening and closing statements. I did all the questioning of witnesses and drew up the jury instructions. Most importantly, the Doc wouldn't testify and promised not to say a word. We figured he could smile at the jury, and if none of them knew him, he might pass for a friendly old geezer.

When the trial rolled around, the government's appraisers testified like professionals, but it wasn't hard to show their bias, due to the number of appraisals they'd made for the Urban Renewal Authority and the large sums they'd been paid for their work. Leon showed a real flair for being the center of attention, and did a good job of deflecting the government attorney's attack on his qualifications. He also hung tenaciously to his opinion that the house was worth $15,000, a princely sum in 1968 and far in excess of the $5,000 value put on the property by the government's witness.

But all this was just preliminary to Ace's testimony. As it turned out, we had saved our best for last. This likable old man was hard to resist. After he identified himself, I asked him a series of questions that went something like this:

Question: "Ace, do you want to sell your house?"
Answer: "Oh, no, Sir, but I have to; they's goin' to taken it."
Question: "Well, Ace, who's goin' to take it?"
Answer: "Da Urban Manure."

Even the Urban Renewal lawyers had to laugh, and when the courtroom finally calmed down, there was no doubt where this case was going. Although, Doyle did overdo his closing argument by goose-stepping across the courtroom and then comparing Urban Renewal to Hitler's Nazi's forcing the Jews out of their homes, our case survived.

The jury didn't take long to bring in a verdict for exactly the value Leon had put on the house. That may not seem like much these days but in the Sixties, it was enough to buy a nice home in a good neighborhood. The law even allowed Ace and the Doc to collect interest, costs, and best of all, attorney's fees. So, everyone came out well in the end.

Well, everyone that is, but Harvey.

A few weeks after the trial, I ran into Doc's ace-in-the-hole. He looked terrible. He had that kind of gray-green color that sick people turn. He had shed twenty or thirty pounds too, but it was clear it wasn't from dieting or taking up running.

"What the hell happened to you, Harvey?" I asked.

"Well, the Doc told me he had mastered the technique of doing a hemorrhoidectomy so that it was completely painless."

At which I point, I blurted out, "You didn't let the Doc operate on you?"

"Yes, and I've never been in so much pain in my life. I had to go to another doctor to get things fixed right. It's been a month now, and it still hurts like hell."

THE TREACHERY OF WOMEN
. . . .

"**W**omen are treacherous," Dale said. We were in the café, like we were almost every morning, gathered for coffee and idle talk. The food wasn't much good but the coffee was hot, and the crowd came mostly to talk anyway, gathered around two linoleum tables, sitting on cheap metal chairs with well-worn red vinyl seats. Advice was free and you got what you paid for that way. Arguments were common and often went on for years, unresolved. Important stuff like who was the first one to date some girl in high school, who scored the winning touchdown in a game decided decades ago, or the worst President ever.

The crowd included a couple of farmers; the operator of the local grain elevator; a lawyer; Dale, an oil and gas landman; and Jack, the local banker. Dale was a tough old dude, with a face like five miles of bad road, who had played linebacker at Tulsa University. Jack had a somewhat benign, almost cherubic look but an ice cold banker's heart. He was a bad gossip who liked to keep abreast of all the local happenings and spent most of his time prying information out of the rest of us. The group gathered was by no means a club and there were no rules, save to be ready to defend yourself at all times, as no one was immune from a well-placed insult or a joke at his expense.

"Of course, women are treacherous," Jack said, "but what are you talking about?"

"Didn't you hear what happened to Rupe?" Dale responded.

"No, don't believe I did," the banker said.

"It's pretty damn funny to everybody but Rupe," said Dale, "and just goes to show that women don't fight fair."

"What happened?" Jack asked.

"You know Stubbs's place over by Seminole?"

"That bar and barbecue joint."

"That's the one."

"What's Rupe got to do with Stubbs?"

"Stubbs got himself one of those Russian women you meet on the Internet. He married her and brought her to the United States. She turned out good. Young, not bad lookin' and didn't mind helpin' Stubbs in the bar. Everybody calls her Olga, I don't even know if that's her real name."

"So what went wrong?" Jack asked.

"Turned out she used to be a gymnast and was strong as hell. Stubbs figured out a way to make some extra money off of her."

"How's that?"

"Guys would come in the bar and get to drinkin', talkin' about how tough they were—you know how guys talk in bars."

"Everybody's bulletproof and undefeated," Jack said.

"Anyway, Stubbs began to bet that Olga could beat 'em at arm wrestling. Of course, none of them fellas would stand for such an insult. Get beat by a girl? No way."

"The thing of it is Olga was not only strong, she was also quick, and had some kind of trick that gave her an advantage. Part of the bet was that she got to stand behind the bar while the guy had to sit on a barstool, so she had more leverage. She embarrassed a lot of big, strong dudes and won Stubbs a bunch of money. Once a guy got beat, he couldn't stand it. He'd go tell a friend about her out and egg him on to see if he could fare better, and then Stubbs would win another bet. There were so many takers, it was like a long congo line."

"So, what happened to Rupe?" asked Jack. "Rupe's the strongest son of a bitch I've ever seen! Hell, I've seen him pick up the back end of a pickup truck and hold it while somebody changed the tire."

"You're right about that, Jack, and being so damn strong is what caused Rupe's problem. Some of the boys heard about Olga and they decided to set old Stubbs up for a big killing. They got him to agree that Olga would take on anyone they could find, and then they talked Rupe into a match. The boys bet it up big with Stubbs."

"The minute Olga and Rupe sat down and Rupe griped Olga's hand, she said knew she had no chance. There wasn't anything she could do to overcome that kind of power. It was like tryin' to stop a bull elephant, but being a woman, that's when she resorted to pure evil, feminine treachery."

"What do you mean by that?" Jack asked.

"Just as Stubbs gave the signal to start, Olga leaned across the bar and French-kissed Rupe. He was so damn flabbergasted, she was able to slam his arm down for the win—she broke a bone in his hand! Of course, all hell broke loose. Stubbs demanded payment, and Rupe's backers refused to pay. Stubbs wouldn't budge, and the losers would have torn the place apart if someone hadn't called the sheriff who cleaned the whole joint out. The whole thing isn't settled yet."

"Never trust a woman," Jack said.

"Don't ever trust a Rusky, either," Dale replied.

BOOTS

. . . .

The gun on the kitchen table was a .45 automatic. The weapon sat next to a half-empty bottle of Jim Beam before Boots, whose black eyes were radiating hatred as I entered. His first words confirmed his mood.

"I'm going to kill the bitch."

I didn't doubt that he meant it.

The bitch in question was Boots's ex-wife, and he made the declaration from his mother's house, the designated exchange point with his ex for their young son, J. Edgar. Only a few minutes before, I had received a frantic call from Boots's mother, begging me to come over as fast as possible and talk to her son who was threatening to kill his ex-wife.

Boots hadn't always been an angry cokehead. He had once been a hipster. Short and thin, his hair styled in a ducktail, Boots had once been known as a jive-talking, wise guy but by day, he was an assistant public defender who prided himself on knowing about all of the deals and conspiracies going on in Oklahoma County, some of them even real.

Boots was way cool, maybe too cool; if you weren't up on the latest slang, it could be hard to follow a conversation with him. A retainer fee was never a thousand dollars but a "yard," or if five hundred dollars, "half a yard." Left and right turns were a "louie" and a "brody." A shrimp cocktail was "six jumbos on ice." In the rare occasion that Boots didn't have a slang word for something, he simply made one up. He also bestowed nicknames on lawyers and judges, so following one of his courtroom stories could be tricky if you didn't know "The Silver Fox," "Fingers," "Little Head," or "His Eminence." Still, Boots would have been just fine if he could have stayed away from the coke, the whiskey, and trashy women, but he couldn't. He put a nail in his marriage by going AWOL for the birth of his son, arriving at the hospital the day *after* the boy was born, only to insist the baby be named J. Edgar. Similar disappearances at work at similarly poor times of his choosing inevitably had led to him losing his public defender job. He had since been reduced to running a somewhat seedy criminal practice, representing a rogues' gallery of lowlifes, most of them charged with drug-related crimes.

Boots also liked to gamble and prided himself on being a good poker player. Word on the street, however, was that he would lay down a bet on almost anything.

It was Boots's gambling that had led to my being in the kitchen of his mother's house on this fine Oklahoma day.

* * * * *

Across the street from the county courthouse and about three blocks from my office, was a barber shop. One of the current barbers, Jack, dubbed "Jacky the Cut" by Boots, was a good barber, popular with lawyers, court reporters, and judges. If I needed a haircut, I would drop by the shop and let Jack know. When he had an opening, he would call my office, and I would hurry over and get trimmed up, before the next customer came into the shop. Remember, this was before cell phones, and so if Jack missed me at the office, I had to try another day.

Although my office was on the ninth floor, one day I was particularly quick getting an elevator and made it over to the barber shop in no more than four or five minutes.

"How the hell did you get here so fast?" Jack said.

"Like the speed of light or a silver bullet," I replied.

My conversation with Jack then drifted to Boots. Boots and Jack played in a weekly poker game where Boots was a consistent winner. They also bet on football games, basketball games, horse races, elections, turtle races, or spelling bees for that matter. The sums they bet weren't a lot; the real benefit of winning was getting to gloat over the victory and ride the other guy until the next bet. Both of them were obnoxious winners but remained friends because they were able to withstand the other's insults without any lasting animus. When Jack started telling me about his latest bet with Boots, an idea sprung to life in my mind.

"You were surprised by how fast I got here from my office weren't you?" I said.

"If I hadn't called you there, I wouldn't have believed it."

"I can get here even faster," I said.

"I don't see how."

"Trust me, I can if I need to."

"What are you saying?" Jack asked.

"Well, you didn't think I could get here that fast. What do you think Boots would think?"

Jack paused a minute, and then we both started laughing.

"So we set Boots up for a bet. I love it!" Jack said.

"No, *you* have to set him up. It has to look as if it wasn't planned. You've got to work him over and get the bet out of him."

"You have an evil mind," Jack said.

"For God's sake, I'm a lawyer. What did you expect!"

We spent the rest of my haircut laughing and planning exactly how we'd frame Boots. The window of time had to be extra tight to get Boots to bet, and the whole thing had to look like Jack's spontaneous idea. The ideal time would be when Boots came in for a scheduled haircut appointment.

I figured, Jack could just tell me in advance, and I would do the rest. First, however, we needed to do some calculations.

Waiting for an elevator and then walking at a brisk pace to the barbershop, usually took me between five and ten minutes. The day that I surprised Jack, I had arrived in under five minutes, a feat made possible by an elevator sitting open on my floor when I left my office. Of course, I intended to run not walk for the bet, but the key to winning the bet was still to have an elevator waiting for me on the ninth floor. This meant I had to talk to Jack on the phone while my associate rushed to the hallway and summoned an elevator. If I could jump into an elevator, hustle through the lobby, and then sprint the three blocks. I was pretty darn sure I could make it under three minutes and for sure, under four. Of course, I couldn't let Boots see me running so I had to walk up to the door of the barbershop at no more than a brisk pace and not huffing and puffing.

We practiced the plan as though it was a fire drill. When the call came from Jack, my secretary would stall. My associate, Mike, would race into the hall, call an elevator to the floor, and hold the elevator door open, fending off any and all comers. Jack was then supposed to casually say that he had an open chair but only if I could come over right away, and with that, I was to take off.

A few weeks passed before Jack let me know Boots was scheduled for a 2:00 p.m. haircut the next day.

I cleared my schedule and the game was on.

Jack's call came in at 2:30 p.m. My secretary put him on hold; Mike scurried to the elevator; and I stalled for a minute or two waiting for the elevator to arrive before I took Jack's call. Jack was a surprisingly good actor; his drop-in haircut offer was delivered in a casual routine way but it might as well have been a gunshot at the local horse races.

I took off for the elevator.

Mike was holding the door open; I jumped in, hit the button, and descended. As luck would have it, there were no intermediate stops between the ninth floor and the ground floor. I was flying as I hit the lobby. I sprinted to the back door of the building and burst out onto the alley in a dead sprint. I've always wondered what was going through the minds of the pedestrians who saw me, a guy in a suit and tie, busting out of an office building in downtown Oklahoma City like he had shot someone. They probably wondered where were the cops chasing me.

With only a glance, I was across Robinson Avenue and flying toward the courthouse. Just short of the corner of Jack's building, I lurched to a stop, took a deep breath, and then casually walked around the corner. I could see Boots in the barber chair and Jack standing behind him, trying not to laugh. When I opened the door, before I could say anything, Boots blurted out, "No fucking way!"

Still out of breath but determined not to show it, I bought a few seconds to calm my vitals by giving him a puzzled look before finally saying, "Hi, Boots, what are you talking about?"

"No fucking way did you get here that fast from your office."

"Don't try and welch," Jack said. "You watched me dial his office and made me let you listen so you'd know he was there. Time to pay up. One hundred now, not later, your credit's no good here."

Still grumbling, Boots pulled out his wallet and handed Jack a hundred dollar bill. At that point, we couldn't stand it any longer. Jack, the other barber, and I burst into laughter. Boots knew then that he had been had.

"Give me my damn money back! You guys set me up!"

"Nope—he was in his office. He got here in less than five minutes. I won the bet fair and square," Jack replied.

"How in the hell can you say fair and square when the son of a bitch is a runner, and he had to run not walk to get here that fast."

And so the argument raged on, until some of us got tired and went home. As far as I know, the bet was never settled.

* * * * *

What did have to be settled was Boots's threat to "kill the bitch." My plan this time was to keep Boots talking, which wasn't hard, and then to just reason with him, which was. Trying to reason with an enraged drunk is never an easy task, and I was pretty sure it wasn't going to work this time either—my reasoning skills weren't anything to brag about. However, I could grab the gun off of the table before Boots stopped me, so that's what I did—and just in time.

He had just started to vent some of his rage on me when the doorbell rang, which meant the ex-wife had arrived with J. Edgar.

Boots jumped up to get to the door first but both his mom and I beat him to it. I had the honor of holding Boots back as he spewed hate at the ex-wife, but no one was too worried about the ex. She didn't think any more of Boots than he did of her, and they dog-cussed each other nonstop while Boots's mom took J. Edgar with her into another room.

No killing was done that night.

As for Boots's relationship with his ex-wife, well, it was already so bad, nothing could have made it any worse. From what the fellas at the barbershop say, things never did get any better between them before he died, which wasn't long thereafter.

Officially, Boots was done in by a "heart attack," which meant probably a drug overdose.

And, yes, I did take Boots's gun home with me that day he went after his ex, and yes, it was loaded.

WEARING OUT THE FREE LAWYER
. . . .

The call came in the same way that it always did, from the judge's clerk. Only, this time, my new involuntary clients were already in the federal penitentiary at El Reno, rather than sitting in the county jail awaiting arraignment in U.S. District Court.

At a time before the federal government saw fit to fund public defenders, indigents charged with federal crimes were defended by members of the local bar, who received no fee for their services. U.S. district judges took this responsibility seriously and expected every lawyer to take a turn when appointed. Since ours was a small district with only three judges, almost no young lawyer had the temerity to attempt to avoid a criminal defense appointment, particularly since such attempts where almost universally unsuccessful and only served to create animosity between them and the appointing judge and his clerk.

Thus, when summoned, I simply asked what the charges were, the names of the defendants, and requested copies of the indictments and any other available information. I quickly learned my clients were charged with attempted murder and assault with a deadly weapon. The pair had supposedly set out to kill one prisoner with a makeshift knife they'd made in prison, and in the process, they attacked a second inmate with a lead pipe. Miraculously, both victims had survived. No bonus for the accused, as the government had listed the victims as witnesses.

This figured to be a case ripe for a plea bargain seeking to add as little time as possible to my clients' present sentences. After all, nobody could get too excited about the victims, a drug dealer and an embezzler. However, it didn't take long for my clients to disabuse me over the thought of any plea bargain.

"Not again. No way. That's why I'm here. Some damn lawyer made a deal," was the first thing I heard from Roy when I introduced the idea of a guilty plea.

"These guys are finks; they won't testify against us. They're scared shitless. If they testify against us, they're dead men."

Roy it turned out was twenty-four years old, and had already spent eight years of his life in prison or juvenile detention.

"What do you do when you're not in jail?" I naively asked.

"Nothin."

"Where do you go?"

"Stay with my cousin in Kansas City."

"What do you do for work?"

"Nothin much.

"Well what do you do all day?"

"Hang out; watch TV."

"How do you get by?"

"I steal cars."

What Roy didn't say—but his record showed—was that Roy was a bad car thief. He stole cars, and got caught, and went to jail. When he got out, he stole cars again, and got caught again, and went to jail again. His life and his society were in prison. He spoke the language of the jailhouse and lived by prison rules. He knew only prison life, and that's what led him to attack the victim who was as he so elegantly put it, a "fink."

In Roy's society, finks *deserved* to die.

In Roy's society, finks *died*, simple as that.

Roy was still young but he was already a hard case. He was dumb and vicious but a sweetheart compared to my other client, Dick. Dick was in solitary. He'd been put there because of repeated attempts to escape and commit suicide. His belt and shoelaces had long before been taken away from him as a basic precaution against further suicide attempts. Dick had come out of solitary confinement only to attempt suicide by underwear—he tied his hands behind his back with his briefs, climbed onto the prison sink, and dove head-first into the concrete cell floor. The suicide failed, but he did manage to dislocate his neck.

Dick's unique suicide attempt had enhanced his long-standing reputation for crazy, a reputation gained from the time he tried to escape from the prison exercise yard in broad daylight. He climbed the prison fence, made it over the razor wire at the top (though not before it cut his hands to shreds), and made a run for freedom. Pinned down by gunfire from guards on the prison wall who let fly a fusillade of bullets, Dick hid in a ditch but, like Roy and his auto heists, none too well. Dick was quickly apprehended and dragged back to prison.

To say Dick was an antisocial psychopath, probably qualified as an understatement. His eyes had an intense, psycho look that always made me alert and uneasy. Of course, Dick was also against any kind of plea bargain. However, unlike Roy, he did have a defense this time, sort of. He had only been identified as a lookout, posted by Roy to watch for guards at the door of a darkened TV room, while Roy attacked the fink. There would likely have only been the one victim but the other victim had made the mistake of trying to help the fink, only to be bludgeoned by Roy, with his alternate weapon of choice, a lead pipe.

Dick swore that he was merely an innocent bystander who had been dragged into the case because he happened to be present and a friend of Roy's, an unlikely story on its face, since Roy had no friends. It was also contrary to the testimony of the victims who would later testify that Dick went to the door of the TV room, signaled an all clear to Roy, and then closed the door and guarded it so they could not escape.

I did have one thing going for me with Dick. He thought I was a great lawyer. This belief was born from my unrelated success in retrieving his supply of comic books from the prison guards. I had made the mistake just before leaving our first visit of asking if there was anything I could do for him.

"Yes, I want my comic books back."

"Who has them?"

"The guards won't let me have my comic books," Dick said.

"Why?"

"I don't know; they just won't."

"We'll see about that."

On my way out of the solitary confinement wing, I approached a somewhat surly guard stationed at the entrance and demanded, "Give him back his comic books; he can't hurt himself with a comic book." After some hemming and hawing, the guard finally produced a pillowcase filled with comic books, and reluctantly delivered them back to Dick in his cell.

* * * * *

After that, in Dick's mind, I was a true legal genius, quite probably, the only person who had ever successfully challenged any authority on his behalf. His confidence in my ability was at best a mixed blessing since he now became more convinced than ever that somehow I would see him found not guilty.

When practicing criminal law, you quickly learn that your client is often your worst enemy, and this case was no exception. Roy continued to insist the victims were too afraid to testify. After all, who would want to remain in prison with the likes of him and Dick after *finking* on them in court? It made sense but not this time. As Roy contemplated his second victory by way of my skills, the assistant U.S. district attorney let me know that one victim had been released early and the other had been moved to a state prison in Michigan to assure his safety. She also took the opportunity to show me the weapon: a shiv constructed by pounding the edge of a metal door hinge into a jagged saw-like blade that resembled a knife. Although the shiv had been found wiped clean of fingerprints in a trash can some distance away from the TV room, it could be traced to Roy's shift in the prison workshop. Naturally, Roy and Dick told me that they knew nothing about the weapon and had never seen it before. They even helped invent the O. J. defense that the knife had been "planted" by evil guards out to get them.

In any event, the only course of action was to plead not guilty, object to everything, and try to create reasonable doubt, or better yet, a reversible legal error by the district attorney, or the judge. Lots of luck, sucker. The judge and the prosecutor had seen assholes like me before. From this unenviable posture, we proceeded to trial before twelve people, hardly peers, as I would not accuse any half-decent citizen of ever having sunk to the level of my clients.

Alas, both victims did appear and testify against the defendants, not without some obvious fear, which only served to make them more credible witnesses. The highlight of their testimony was the unveiling of the one fink's fiery scar, which stretched from his chest to below his belly button. The vicious-looking knife that made it and my client's appearance didn't help matters. I could, like John Grisham or Gerry Spence, regale you with how my brilliant legal maneuvering brought about an unlikely acquittal but in the interest of historical accuracy, and in this case justice, suffice to say that I did raise every objection both known and previously unknown, vociferously argued reasonable doubt and even convinced myself Dick might be innocent.

But the jury found both defendants guilty on all charges.

After the clerk announced the verdict of guilty, I requested that the jury be polled. Each juror was then required to state his or her vote, verbally in open court. Although, this seldom changes the verdict, it can in rare cases lead to some equivocation on the part of a juror that can set up the grounds for a mistrial. This hope was quickly dashed as each member of the jury stood, one by one, and responded with an emphatic "Guilty!" Doing so despite in each case, Dick leveling his index finger as if it were a gun and pretending to click off a fatal shot at the responding juror.

In the aftermath of that foolishness, I turned to Roy, who was seated next to me, to advise him that his sentence would be up to the judge. Before I could, he proclaimed in a loud voice, "I'll kill the first son of a bitch that says anything!" Choosing not to be that son of a bitch, I kept my mouth shut. The U.S. marshals also heard Roy's threat, and taking no chances, quickly jerked his arms behind his chair and handcuffed him.

That was that. The poor, dear boys were sentenced to another ten years each and returned to their home away from home at El Reno. Unfortunately, I had a duty to tell them they had a right to appeal their case to the Tenth Circuit Court of Appeals. Although I advised them there appeared to be no reversible error in the record, I'm sure you know already what they wanted, since free legal services were available and their status in prison was at stake.

Tough guys always appeal.

Anything for a chance at a change of scenery.

* * * * *

I did my job as the American legal system required. I studied long and hard and wrote the best brief possible, introducing the knife was prejudicial, the evidence was insufficient as to Dick, etcetera, etcetera, etcetera. At least, I figured that I would get a trip to Denver to argue some of my etceteras (the government did pay for travel and per diem). Wrong, again, the circuit court simply affirmed the original verdict without even hearing oral argument.

At last, the case was over, or so I thought. Once again, I had to advise my clients they could appeal to the U.S. Supreme Court; although, there were no odds long enough to express their chance of success. Of course, the boys wanted to appeal but it would not be with me as their lawyer, thank the Lord, since I wasn't admitted to practice before the U.S. Supreme Court at the time, a fact I proudly announced to the judge's clerk. "Well, that's not the way it works," the clerk responded. "You prepare the Petition for Certiorari to the Supreme Court even though you're not admitted."

Swell, another futile brief for no pay and for a client who kept shooting himself in the proverbial foot, but at least I finally got something out of the case besides this story. At the time, Justice William O. Douglas had suffered a severe stroke but was refusing to resign from the U.S. Supreme Court. Any decision he took part in was subject to challenge by the losing side because of this, and so a legal debate was raging over the issue.

Thus, the Order denying Certiorari, the inevitable decision of even the Warren Court, carried a stamped legend: "Justice Douglas took no part in this decision." A small footnote to history, which I still have in my files.

There is also a postscript to this story.

Not too long after this case, I tried a hotly contested, and very technical, lien foreclosure case before the same judge. The case was close and involved a lot of money and one of my best clients. My client prevailed and was entitled to have the loser, a title insurance company, pay my attorney's fee. I filed a fee application for a fair and reasonable fee. In lawyer's parlance, this means the very most money you could ever dream of sticking to the other side. Sometime after filing, I got another call from the judge's clerk. Oh no, I thought, not another free criminal appointment, but instead the clerk informed me: "The judge looked at your attorney's fee application. He didn't think it was enough for the work you had to do because the other side filed so many motions and prolonged the trial. He added a bonus fee to what you requested, and by the way, he wanted me to thank you for all the time you spent defending those two little scumbags at El Reno."

PAUL

· · · · · · · · · · · ·

Paul Smith was average in almost every way. He was of average height and average weight. His appearance was average, with brown hair, brown eyes, and unremarkable features. His voice was unforgettable and so was his presence. The man was simply not memorable in any way but one.

Paul was good with numbers. No, he was great with numbers. Actually, he was exceptional with numbers. In high school, Paul was a C student, except in math. In math, he was a wizard, making straight A's without even trying. After high school, he joined the Army, where, amazingly, the U.S. Army recognized Paul's talent and assigned him to work in information technology. Before long, Paul was at the Pentagon creating computer programs to correlate intelligence data collected by satellites.

After Paul got out of the service, he returned to his hometown of Lansing, Michigan. He married a young woman who worked for the State of Michigan in the treasurer's office. Paul used the G.I. Bill to go to a community junior college and zipped through college in a little over one year, earning a degree in computer science. Several teachers remarked that Paul knew more about computers than they did. While still in college, Paul had applied for a job with the Michigan State Election Board. The interviewer was impressed with Paul's IT experience, and it helped that he was a veteran. He was hired, and soon made responsible for organizing and programming the electronic counting of votes in the state. His work was impeccable, and no one ever questioned his expertise; no one, that is before the presidential election of 2020.

On November 10, 2020, after having worked almost eighteen hours a day for more than a week, Paul was rechecking the final vote count when his boss, the Secretary of State, appeared in the office. The Secretary of State was an old Republican warhorse. In his sixties, the secretary had spent his entire life in Republican politics, either in appointed or elected offices. An affable man, with a reputation for honesty, he had many friends and few enemies. Paul, on the other hand, was a man with only an average interest in politics at best and a registered Independent. Paul usually voted but held no strong political ideology.

"Paul, the Trump campaign is accusing me of fraud and failure to follow the law. I have to have a press conference to refute their charges," the secretary said.

"They don't know what they are talking about," said Paul. "We worked our asses off to make sure the election was fair."

"I know, I know, but I want you to come with me in case they have any technical questions," the secretary said.

So Paul agreed to appear with the Secretary of State at the press conference. The press conference was well attended and covered by all of the local television channels. The secretary read a prepared statement setting out all of the precautions that had been taken by his office to ensure an accurate vote count. He specifically refuted each and every accusation made by Trump's lawyers, and then took questions from the press. During the question period, the secretary introduced Paul, and Paul responded to some of the more technical questions. Having never been on TV before, he was nervous, but he did, as one would expect, average. His statements discredited all of the allegations of fraud made by Trump and his lawyers, some of which were ridiculous. After the press conference, the Secretary thanked him for participating and Paul returned to his office, to continue his work, with his usual diligence.

The next evening, Paul got to leave work at a normal time. He drove home to an average, middle-class, suburban neighborhood.

As Paul pulled into his driveway he waived to his neighbor, Ted, who was raking leaves in his yard. Ted still had a "Trump, Pence" sign in his yard. Paul got out of his car and started toward his house. He was thinking about having a beer and watching some television and was startled when a big SUV pulled into his driveway and parked behind his car. Four bearded men got out of the SUV. All four men were dressed in a paramilitary fashion, wearing camo, boots, and either ball caps or campaign caps.

As the four men approached Paul, they spread out around him in a rough semicircle. One man stepped forward. He was tall and heavy with a bit of a beer gut and a thick, black beard.

"You're Paul Smith," the tall man said.

"Yes. What do you want?" Paul replied.

"You are a traitor," the same man said.

"I don't know what you are talking about," Paul replied.

"Listen, Motherfucker, you know you stole the election from Trump. You liberal son of a bitch."

Paul turned and headed for his front door but before he could take more than a few steps, he was grabbed from behind, jerked around, and thrown to the ground. Paul started to scramble to his feet but a vicious kick to his side left him crumpled back on the ground. He rolled away from the attack but not in time to avoid another kick that caught him in the thigh. As Paul tried once more to struggle to his feet, one of the other men stepped forward and threw a roundhouse punch at Paul's head. Paul partially ducked the blow but the punch still caught the side of his skull, sending him back to his knees.

"Tell that cocksucker you work for we're coming for him," the tall man said.

The men then turned and climbed back into the SUV. Two of them were laughing but they all looked pleased with their work. The SUV backed out of the driveway, turned, and drove away, never facing in a direction where Paul could see the license number.

Paul was dazed and thought a rib was broken. He tried to get up and someone extended him a helping hand.

It was his neighbor, Ted.

"What in the hell happened?" Ted said.

"Some of your good ol' boys," Paul grunted.

"That's not right," Ted said.

THE POEMS

Susan Bodtke
Sulfur Spring, OKLA

COMMITTEES

Investigate the causes,
consider the options,
discuss the consequences,
analyze the alternatives,
define the parameters,
predict the results,
categorize the components,
review the reasons,
weigh the outcome,
scrutinize the details,
confront the criticisms,
study the particulars,
compromise the controversies,
eliminate the objections,
renumber the paragraphs,
comment on the coffee,
debate the merits,
sharpen the pencils,
and,
do absolutely nothing.

EULOGIES

They were all great men
when they died,
as though the inevitable act of dying
made them great,
somehow absolving them of
their normal mediocrity,
when they were
neither great nor small,
just men.

COYOTE

I've seen Dixie come
and Dixie go
and said goodbye to Jesus.

I'm standing on a
railroad track
in southern Arizona,
watching a coyote run, and
he's headed for the border.

Where cactus, clouds, and cougars
dwell
and there isn't any water.

Where hope is North
and guns decide
and sand goes on
forever.

Where life is cheap,
and death is close
and mercy granted
never.

THE SPY

He hears things
that have never
been heard.

He sees things
that shouldn't
be seen.

He knows things
that no one should
know.

He may be the
ultimate spy
or have a bad
case of paranoia.

GHOSTS

Have you ever been in a prairie storm
    straight from Hell where tornadoes are born,

Rain clouds rising, black and wild,
    wind that sounds like the Devil's own child,

Sometimes in these storms appear,
    Indian ghosts that white men fear

Headdress, war paint, shield and lance,
    shrouded by rain on the prairies' expanse

Riding the storm on lightning flashes,
    galloping through these barren places

Charging, twisting, running hard,
    breaking through realities' guard

Born on wind that's wild and free,
    fearsome reminders of history

Laying waste to white men's lands,
    plucked by force from Indians' hands

Control regained by mythical forces
assaulting time on spirit horses

For an instant years reversed
storm fulfilling bloody thirst

Taking scalps on settlers' farms
wind and rain the warriors' arms.

CAP'N TOM

Here's to you, Cap'n Tom
who saw death
dealt out
in a hundred different ways
and who survived two wars,
not just the Great One.

Although, the chickenshits
in Washington called one
a "Police Action."
Policing what?
A frozen piece of Hell
so cold they wouldn't even
tell you the temperature.

A place,
where you and your buddies
slaughtered Chinese by the
thousands,
and soldiers gave their lives
for Hyundai cars, women golfers,
and to make it safe
for the world's cruelest dictator.

At least, you had those years
in a sunny place,
to fish each day,
without death
standing in your way.

Now you rest in peace.
No hero's death for you,
but by God, a soldier
through and through.

ONCE A YEAR

Once a year
I go to church.
My mom,
a regular, herself,
likes for me
to take her
on Easter.
It helps out
the preacher,
who gets to make
snide remarks
about me and the
other sinners who,
only come,
once a year.
Although I suspect
some of them cheat
and come
on Christmas too.
I've made
my peace
with God
about it.

He knows
I come
for my mom,
not for him, and
don't take
him for a fool,
who might
be persuaded
by my showing up,
once a year.

THE COLDEST SPOT IN HELL

I won't get to heaven
it's a fate
that I know well
I'd just like
to settle for
the coldest spot in Hell

A little air-conditioning
would suit me
just swell
when things get hot
down under in
the coldest spot in Hell

There are sins
that I've admitted
and ones
that I won't tell
but none are bad enough
for me to lose
the coldest spot in Hell

I've never been to prison
or locked up in a cell
nothing that should
keep me from
the coldest spot in Hell

When you consider Hitler
and of Charlie Manson tell
it looks like
I'm entitled to
the coldest spot in Hell

So when I get
to where I'm goin'
I'll be staying
for a spell
so hold my reservation for
the coldest spot in Hell

THE KING'S JUGGLER

He called himself a juggler
and he juggled for the king
he called himself a juggler
and he could juggle anything.

He could juggle wives and knives
and even pigs with wings
he called himself a juggler
and he could juggle anything.

He could juggle hearts and darts
and things both big and small
he called himself a juggler
who could juggle anything at all.

He juggled words and flying birds
and thoughts that others had
he called himself a juggler
and could juggle good and bad.

He could juggle bats and hats
and even vicious, screaming cats
he called himself a juggler
and could juggle round and flat.

He could juggle Chinese gongs
and stanzas from forgotten songs
he called himself a juggler
and could juggle short or long.

He could juggle flying plates
and college students and their dates
he called himself a juggler
sometimes early, sometimes late.

He could juggle moving cars
and from the heavens a falling star
he called himself a juggler
and he juggled near and far.

And no matter how he juggled
he disappeared in air
and the place where he had juggled
was just no longer there.

And the King looked for his juggler
he found an empty place
the juggler he had juggled,
long gone in time and space.

YES, BUT . . .

I love you, but . . .
I love another more
You're doing, fine, but
I'll show you out the door

But, is something
you wish was never said
But, is something
that works inside your head

I'll make that loan you wanted, but
there's something you must do
it's not as though the animals
get to run the zoo

It's a word that's made to weasel
and it's always qualified, but
it's better to have used it
then to just flat out have lied

But, may be considered
just another bland conjunction
But, always leads
to some serious dysfunction

But, whatever picture
this idea may provoke
But, may be remembered
as a signal or a joke

and, but may be less useful
than the poet thinks
because you may discover
                this poem's missing link

THE SCIENTIST

He could see
down long roads
and around corners
where the crazy ghosts
told forgotten stories
in the strange half light
that never existed

He could touch
untouchable things
and even hold them
in his hand,
like a god,
without fear

He knew
the turbulence of times
and the questions
that had no answers

Finally, he saw
that place in space
where time
and light
intersect
to disappear
all substance
known and unknown,
to man

WINTER

Two fat ladies walking
rotund and robust
bundled against the cold

A lone runner
tall and thin
dressed in black
slicing through a gray sky

Do the men and the women
killed by random road rage
care whether their murderer
was a Muslim terrorist?

If you posted on Facebook
that you were going to commit suicide
how would your "friends" react?

What makes hate
so attractive?

Damn that
Oklahoma wind

I wish it was
summer again.

MEMORIAL DAY

Here lies a soldier.
He lived too long.

He came back from the war
but he never came home
from the jungle where
he left his soul and most of his mind.

The enemy couldn't kill him
but the war did.

Dying is easy.
Living is hard,
when you're dealt the joker
as your last card.

A DEVIL'S WELCOME

I dreamed all of the hypocrites
were standing in line
at the gates of Hell.

All of the sanctimonious Bible thumpers,
with their, *Have a blessed day.*

All of the draft-dodging war mongers,
with their, *Thank you for your service.*

All of the fake tough guys,
with their, *I'll bomb the hell out of them.*

All of the lying politicians,
with their, *It'll be the biggest, the greatest,
the longest, the strongest,
the mostest, the toastest for everyone.*

Ever a diabolically clever old cuss,
the devil knew what to do;
he made them look
at their dead bodies, all the
abused and neglected children,
all the dead soldiers,
all the millions of civilians killed
in the name of someone's god.

It didn't change a damned one of them.

WHATEVER HAPPENED TO . . .

The girl I met
in the bar in Checotah
who looked like she
should be in Vegas?

The headmaster who
wanted to throw the
whole basketball team
out of school but didn't
have the guts?

The California cop
who cut me a break
when I needed it?

The vending machine
supplier that
disappeared when
the mob hit town?

The relative
who tipped
me off that my
client was lying?

Maybe, I don't want
to know.

WHO'LL WRITE THE POEMS

Who'll write the poems
when the poets are gone
Who'll write the sonnets
Who'll write the songs

Who'll tell the tales
of love won and love lost
of victories in battle
and total the cost

Who'll fill the pages
with words and with rhymes
Who'll tease history
and speak of the times

Who'll trumpet the praises
of saints and of sinners
Who'll be the judge
of losers and winners

Poets sing anthems
and poets are blind
making a wreck out
of distance and time

Playing with words
meant only for fools
stumbling along without
any rules

So tell a good story
or sing a sad song

KINGS

In the land
of the blind,
a one-eyed man
is King

In the land
of one-eyed men,
there are
no Kings

In the land
of Kings,
all men
are blind

THE LAWYER

A lawyer died today.
They say he passed away,
without a sound.
I know that it's not true,
for it would never do,
for even God
to have the last word.
He left little estate, and
only one last wish,
to be buried standing up,
so that he'd arrive in Hell
ready to give
his opening statement
to the devil.

ACKNOWLEDGMENTS

I want to thank my friend Patrick Riley for agreeing to illustrate this book. As you can easily see, Patrick is a terrific artist and is just as talented as a sculptor and mask maker. I hope my stories can live up to his drawings.
I would also like to thank the readers of my newsletter "Common Sense" who motivate me to keep writing.

ABOUT THE AUTHOR

Kent Frates is an Oklahoma City attorney, historian, and author. He served in the Oklahoma Legislature from 1970 to 1978. The editor and publisher of the political and literary newsletter "Common Sense," he is the author of the poetry book *The Captain and His Crew*, the novel *Don't Never Shoot Short*, and four works of nonfiction, including *Oklahoma Hiking Trails*, *Oklahoma Courthouse Legends*, and *Oklahoma's Most Notorious Cases*, Volumes 1 and 2. A contributor to both *This Land* and *Oklahoma Today* magazine, Frates wrote the original script for the independent film *CockFight*, which was filmed in Oklahoma, starring Wilford Brimley, Rex Linn, and Gailard Sartain.

Oklahoma's Most Notorious Cases won the national 2015 Benjamin Franklin Award for political and current events.